"Our problem is that we're a lot alike, you and I. Both of us are too proud to accept help," her boss said.

"You're in charge of a murder investigation, you've got trauma that gives you nightmares and it seems a killer is focused on you." Cassie planted her hands on her hips. "Sorry if I thought I should spare you."

"Because I couldn't handle it."

Her eyes burned fire. "No, because I care about you."

She turned to leave, but Max caught her arm and pulled her against his chest. As he looked into wide blue eyes, he lost himself for a second, forgetting where he was and who she was and...

...he kissed her. Just like that.

And she tasted heavenly.

PAT WHITE

the
AMERICAN
TEMP

and the
BRITISH
INSPECTOR

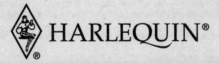
HARLEQUIN®

TORONTO • NEW YORK • LONDON
AMSTERDAM • PARIS • SYDNEY • HAMBURG
STOCKHOLM • ATHENS • TOKYO • MILAN • MADRID
PRAGUE • WARSAW • BUDAPEST • AUCKLAND

Thanks to Sue Heneghan of the Chicago PD,
and FBI Agent Mike Johnson for the law enforcement
info, and thanks to Michelle Tucker-Findlay
for the scoop on the great city of Chicago.

ISBN-13: 978-0-373-69235-4
ISBN-10:   0-373-69235-8

THE AMERICAN TEMP AND THE BRITISH INSPECTOR

Copyright © 2007 by Pat White

www.eHarlequin.com

Printed in U.S.A.

ABOUT THE AUTHOR

Growing up in the Midwest, Pat White has been spinning stories in her head ever since she was a little girl, stories filled with mystery, romance and adventure. Years later, while trying to solve the mysteries of raising a family in a house full of men, she started writing romance fiction. After six Golden Heart nominations and a *Romantic Times BOOKreviews* Award for Best Contemporary Romance (2004), her passion for storytelling and love of a good romance continues to find a voice in her tales of romantic suspense. Pat now lives in the Pacific Northwest, and she's still trying to solve the mysteries of living in a house full of men—with the added complication of two silly dogs and three spoiled cats. She loves to hear from readers, so please visit her at www.patwhitebooks.com.

Books by Pat White

CAST OF CHARACTERS

Max Templeton—Former chief inspector for the Special Crimes Initiative at Scotland Yard, Max was wounded in a terrorist bombing a year ago. Now he's being asked to lead a team of private investigators to catch a London serial killer who has resurfaced in the States.

Cassie Clarke—Max's temporary assistant. Hired to help him with his tell-all crime novel, Cassie struggles with a dark past of her own.

The Blackwell Group:

Jeremy Barnes—Max's second-in-command at Scotland Yard, Jeremy was on the fast track, hoping for Max's job. Only, he didn't expect to get it by default.

Bobby Finn—A former juvenile delinquent, Bobby was taken under Max's wing.

Art McDonald—Bobby's partner.

Ruth Kreeger—Forensics specialist who has solved high-profile serial cases.

Eddie Malone—Computer geek extraordinaire.

Joe Spinelli—Former Chicago police detective hired by the family of a murdered boy.

The Crimson Killer—London serial killer who has presumably taken the lives of two college students in Chicago.

Chapter One

Black smoke burned his eyes and strangled his lungs. Cries for help tore at his heart, begging, pleading. He had to get up, but couldn't feel his legs.

How many would die because he couldn't move or phone for help? Because he was pinned in place, weakened by the explosion?

Maniacal laughter hummed in his ears. Hummed, then echoed, then burst his eardrums with unbearable pain. Pain that was nothing compared to the heaviness clenching his chest.

His fault. They'd die because of him.

He searched the dense mass of nothingness. Had to see, had to make note of every detail, every nuance. His eyes fixed on black. Black with no shape or definition, black that hovered dangerously close.

It was his turn now. His turn to die…

"Wake up!"

A woman's voice shook the breath from him. God, where was he and how did he get here?

He struggled to breathe, every muscle in his body strung taut with fear. Bright light streamed through a window. He blinked.

"What…where am I?" He swallowed back the panic.

"Shh. You're okay," a woman said. "You're home, remember?"

"London?"

"Seattle."

That's right, he'd run away, thousands of miles to another country.

"Cassie?" he said. Cassie, his assistant, his nurse.

"It's me. You're fine. You had a bad dream."

She put her hand on his shoulder and the warmth of human touch set off an explosion in his chest. He jerked away, swung his legs over the other side of the bed and planted his feet on the floor. He snatched his cane from the wall and stood. *Steady now, steady.*

"You're here early," he said.

"It's nine."

And you're a bastard.

She didn't say it, but he heard it in her voice. And she was right. He was a bastard.

She stood in his bedroom, surveying the most intimate place in his flat. She knew everything about him: that he wore silk boxers, not briefs, kept a glass of water by his bed, along with bottles of Halcion and

Vicodin. Yet she was nothing more than hired help, contracted to take dictation and keep him focused.

He grabbed the pack from the nightstand and lit a fag. His fingers trembled, bugger. Trembled like an old woman's.

"You should really quit smoking," she said.

"Yes, Mummy."

She marched off into the living room, footsteps echoing on the hardwood. He'd aggravated her again.

Bad move, Max. You can't afford to lose this one.

He'd already gone through two assistants, neither of them willing to put up with his surly nature. Some might even call it abusive.

He stretched out his neck. Only then did he remember he'd slept starkers because of his night sweats.

He glanced over his shoulder and took a long drag. She'd found him screaming in his sleep, stark naked, and all she could do was scold him for smoking. There'd been no spark of awareness, no sexual attraction. No temptation to touch him in any way but motherly comfort.

Sure, right. He was a cripple. The only feeling a woman could muster was pity.

"Scrambled eggs or over easy?" she called.

He didn't answer, hoping she'd go away. He'd awakened in a foul mood and couldn't deal with her cheerful nature.

"Well?" she said from the doorway.

"I'm not hungry," he said.

Let her make you eggs, fool.

"Tough, I'm making them anyway," she said.

He turned to continue their verbal sparring, but the words caught in his throat. He realized he'd completely exposed himself to her.

Her sweet face showed no reaction, no shock or mild interest.

"I didn't have time to eat this morning so I'm making breakfast," she explained. "Scrambled or over easy?"

She looked quite fetching with her blond hair loose about her shoulders and her cheeks made rosy from the walk over. She never wore much makeup, but then, a girl like Cassie didn't need it.

"Well?" She tapped her foot against the hardwood floor.

"Scrambled."

She disappeared from the doorway and he heard the refrigerator door opening, then closing, an egg cracking, then another.

He glanced outside. A sunny day in rainy Seattle.

He made his way to the bathroom, wondering if a trip to the doctor was in order. He had to get some sleep, but the nightmares made it impossible for him to get more than three hours at a time.

He turned on the water, then tossed his ciggie into the toilet and took a piss.

Only venturing out when absolutely necessary, he'd grown comfortable in his flat. He'd grown comfortable with isolation.

Thank God Brighton Publishing had made him an offer, providing him with moderate financial stability. Max had developed quite a reputation during his days as leader of the Special Crimes Initiative for Scotland Yard, a team created to track elusive serial killers. His experience and reputation had led Brighton to make Max an offer to write a book, a "tell all," the editor had said, "Really gruesome stuff."

Gruesome, like the one that got away?

Not waiting for the water to warm, Max stepped under the cool shower, the spray pounding against his face and chest.

His editor would be pleased with Max's progress so far, and Max was pleased with the wages. There weren't many jobs for a retired detective fighting post-trauma issues, who hadn't solved the biggest case of his career. If only he'd had more time. If only he hadn't lost his grip after the bombing. He was sure that's what the boys at Scotland Yard had whispered when his back was turned: their leader had gone mad.

Bloody hell, they had medication to help him sleep and to ease the healing ache of a shattered hip, but no drugs seemed to help Max's case of post-traumatic stress syndrome. He had a unique case of it, doctors had said. It would take time.

In other words, Max was succumbing to a mysterious mental ailment. He was weak and pathetic. Maybe his biggest critic, Charles Edmonds, was right after all.

A knock interrupted his self-condemnation. "What is it?"

Cassie cracked open the door. "You have a visitor."

"What? At this time of day?"

"He says he's a work associate. He's joining us for breakfast. Hurry, we're getting hungry."

"Now wait a minute—"

The door closed on his protest. She was his employee, hired to listen and type, make grammatical corrections when necessary. He didn't pay her twenty dollars an hour for American female attitude.

He rinsed and dried off. Had someone from Brighton Publishing been sent to check on his progress? But the book wasn't due for five months. He hoped they hadn't uncovered his tangle with Jim Beam last year. He'd been seduced by the devilish malt, but had regained ground and was fully on the mend, at least with the bottle.

He ran his hand across his face, studying his reflection in the mirror. He wasn't prepared for visitors. He hadn't shaved in months, his beard scraggly and untrimmed. A terrible impression to make on a publishing executive.

"Ironed shirts," he muttered, limping across his room and putting on his boxers, then a pair of jeans. He found a shirt still in plastic from the dry cleaners. He slipped it on and grabbed a pair of black trainers.

Someone knocked on the door.

"In a minute!" he called.

Button up. Tuck in neatly…belt…screw the belt, shoes tied…run fingers through hair. Done.

With a hand to the doorknob, he rolled his neck.

He opened the bedroom door and aimed for the kitchen. "Good morning," he said, turning the corner.

"Hello, guv'nor."

Max stopped short at the sight of Jeremy Barnes settled at the kitchen table like a family friend. That sonofabitch.

"Get the hell out of here," Max demanded.

"Mr. Templeton!" Cassie scolded.

"It's okay," Barnes said. "He wasn't expecting me."

"Didn't you hear me?" Max stepped closer to the man who'd been a thorn in his side at SCI, the man who'd quite deftly taken Max's job.

"Good to see you, too, sir."

"What the hell are you doing in my flat?"

"Apartment," Cassie corrected.

"You can leave, too," Max spat out. He didn't mean it, but frustration made him lash out at her as well.

"Breakfast is ready," she said, fiddling with the gold locket at the base of her neck. "I have errands to run."

She went from the kitchen to the front door. Too fast. He wanted her to slow down, to stay and to eat her breakfast.

"I won't be long," she said. "Looks like you two need some privacy."

The door slammed, jarring his teeth. Blast, he was going to chase this one away, too.

"Nice girl," Barnes said.

Max turned to his unwanted guest. "Leave. Now."

"What, and miss breakfast?"

He took a step toward Barnes, figuring to grab hold of the bloke's arm and drag him to the door. Max might be a cripple but he stayed in excellent shape. He could still beat the crap out of Barnes, even if he was a black belt.

"Get out, you toff." He grabbed Barnes's upper arm, wrenching it away from feeding himself.

"Hang on. She makes good scramblers."

"You're eating her breakfast!"

"Eggs will be cold by the time she gets back," Barnes said.

Max squeezed Barnes's arm with one hand and pointed toward the door with the other. "Out!"

"I can't. I need your help."

"What?" Max released his grip.

"You heard me."

"Just got out of the shower. My ears are clogged. Say it again." The left side of his lips curled. A foreign feeling.

"We're in a mess and need your help."

"Well, isn't that bloody amazing? SCI needs help from a cripple."

"I'm not with SCI anymore and you're not a cripple," He paused. "Except in the personality department."

Smart aleck. Barnes was on the fast track to leading a team of his own at Scotland Yard. Max's resignation had made that possible.

Then why was he here, sitting in Max's Seattle kitchen, no longer with SCI?

Max sat down at the table, steepled his fingers and waited. It had been over a year since he'd seen his nemesis from SCI. The bloke hadn't changed much, still tall and lean with trim ash-blond hair and rimless glasses that gave him an air of authority.

More like arrogance. Barnes had always acted superior, as though his university degree had given him the right to look down on the rest of the team at SCI.

Today Barnes's expressionless face told nothing, but the tension oozing from his body revealed plenty. He didn't want to be here.

"Say it again," Max taunted.

"What?"

"Why you've come."

"Your eggs are getting cold. I'll heat them in the micro."

The chair legs scratched against the wood floor as Barnes got up to heat Max's plate. Now he was waiting on Max?

"You're stalling," Max pushed.

"Think so?"

Seconds passed. Fifteen. Thirty. The microwave beeped.

"She's a good cook." Barnes slid the plate in front of Max. "I wouldn't lose her if I were you."

"I won't. I pay her enough."

"Pay her?"

"She's my assistant. What did you think? Forget about Cassie. Come on, say the magic words so we can get on with it."

"Get on with what?"

"You asking for help and me rejecting you."

"Still the same Max Templeton, so sure of yourself, so sure about everything."

If only Barnes could see him waking from a deep sleep, drenched in sweat, calling out for help.

"I'm a busy man," Max said. "If you've got something to say, out with it."

"We need your help."

"We?"

"The Blackwell Group."

Max tipped his head, waiting.

"We're an independent team of investigators who have come together to track down a serial killer. Our team is privately funded—quite well, I might add."

"By whom?"

"He prefers to remain anonymous."

"Very cloak-and-dagger."

"Maybe," Barnes hesitated. "But Blackwell gives us the chance to do things we never could through government channels. It gives us a chance to think outside the box."

To break the rules in order to catch a killer. Max heard the implication.

They ate in silence, a surge of excitement pumping

through Max's blood. To be back in the thick of it, drunk with adrenaline from piecing together a vile criminal act, catching the monster and locking him up.

"We get to pick our team," Barnes said, probably to entice Max further. "Anyone we want. I've contacted a few of the boys from SCI—Bobby Finn and Art McDonald. They took two weeks leave to help us out."

"And after that?" Max said.

"We've got two weeks."

"You're joking?"

"No. The background work's been done on this case. We need to move forward."

"Back in London?"

"No, two murders have occurred in the States—Chicago. Local and federal agencies are baffled. No one can catch him."

More people will die.

Max took a sip of strong coffee. Cassie made great coffee, just this side of bitter.

"Interested?" Barnes asked.

That one word flooded Max with emotion. He wasn't over it, he never would be. Deep down in his soul Max would always be an investigator.

A weak and damaged investigator suffering from a mysterious mental disease. *Back to reality, old chap.*

"So, you want me on your team?" Max said.

"I need you to lead the team. We need your experience."

His experience, knowledge and cunning instinct were

skills that had made Max a top-notch investigator…in his previous life.

He pushed to his feet. Leaning on his cane he swiped his plate from the table, sending his fork flying across the room. "You shouldn't have come." He slammed his plate into the sink, banging it against another dish. "Piss off, and don't step foot in here again."

"Listen, Max—"

"Don't act like we're mates, you bloody hypocrite. All you wanted from me was my job. And you got it, didn't you? You and Charles Edmonds were the end of me."

"He was frustrated that we couldn't find his son's murderer."

"He had me so bloody distracted about losing my job I couldn't do it properly. Maybe if I had been a little more focused I would have seen something at King's Cross and could have prevented that disaster."

"You can't possibly blame yourself for that."

But he did. He blamed himself for not being at the top of his game and not noticing something out of place.

"The Blackwell Group needs you," Jeremy said.

"Bugger off!"

Barnes stood. "Think about it. I'm leaving my mobile number on the counter."

Max followed him to the door, adrenaline pumping through his veins.

"One last thing…" Barnes hesitated. "The killer we're after? Chicago Police think it may be the Crimson Killer."

Heat burned Max's cheeks. More young men were dying because Max hadn't caught a murderer. Barnes no doubt enjoyed seeing Max's reaction to that bit of information.

He pulled open the door, shoved Barnes into the hallway and slammed it shut. Fisting his hands tighter than he thought possible, he pounded on the heavy oak. "Bloody hell."

JEREMY GLANCED at Templeton's door and smiled. Mission accomplished. He descended the stairs to the street front, popped open his mobile and called in.

"It's Barnes."

"How did it go?" the Patron asked.

"He'll do it." He glanced over his shoulder at the flat window. "He can't help himself."

"You believe he's up to it?"

"Yes, sir," Jeremy said without hesitation. He owed his former boss this opportunity.

"But his condition…"

"He's managing." At least Jeremy hoped he was.

"Fine, get on with it. You've got twenty-four hours to finish assembling your team."

"Yes, sir." He hung up.

He'd have to give Max a few hours to cool off. Jeremy had expected as much. Max not only resented Jeremy's ambition, but also his upper-class background and Oxford education. Jeremy's parents had planned on him becoming a solicitor, but he'd wanted to be a police detective. His family had never recovered from that one, their black-sheep son.

Jeremy's ambition and the fact he'd taken Max's job when he'd left SCI, had made Max dislike Jeremy even further. Max wouldn't join the Blackwell Team willingly.

But with the possibility of the Crimson Killer on the loose, the seeds of frustration would grow wild until Max couldn't stand it. He'd have to shelve the pride and cope with his PTSD in order to solve this case and make things right.

Making things right was Jeremy's goal in offering this position to Max. He owed his surly ex-boss as much. If Jeremy hadn't been stuck in traffic, Max wouldn't have been at King's Cross when the bomb went off. Instead, Jeremy would have been blown across the train station, his career would have been over, and he'd be hiding in a flat somewhere, unable to deal with the trauma.

He glanced at the flat window. How bad was it, he wondered? Max could use an ally, someone to stick by his side and help him cope. He sure as hell wouldn't accept help from Jeremy.

Max was a brilliant investigator and knew the C.K. case better than anyone. Offering him this position felt justified, it felt good. Jeremy hadn't felt good about much since the bombing. Guilt had been his unwelcome companion this past year.

He made some calls while he waited for the girl to return, calls to solidify his team. Time was against them, but with an expert group, Jeremy felt sure they could solve the case.

About twenty minutes later, Max's assistant bounded up the sidewalk toward the flat. She had a lightness about her, an innocence. He sensed something between Max and the blond girl that even Max seemed oblivious to. The most important lesson Jeremy had learned from his boss: key clues are often right in front of you.

She approached Jeremy. "What happened? Did he kick you out?"

"Afraid so."

"Too bad. He could use the company to practice his social skills."

Yes, she was perfect.

"How long have you been with Max?" he asked.

"Started working for him about four months ago."

"Doing?"

"Transcribing his book, picking up around the apartment, light cooking, errands. I guess you'd call me his Girl Friday."

"He's a demanding boss, I'll bet."

"Pretty much."

"But you haven't quit."

"I need the money."

And he needs you.

"Cassie, is it?"

"Yes."

Jeremy shot her a charming smile. "How do you feel about travel?"

Chapter Two

Max fought back overwhelming panic and climbed out of the cab, leaning heavily on his cane. What the hell was he doing here? A mistake. He never should have come.

He stood on the Chicago sidewalk and studied the old brick building aged with charm. This would be the command center and his home for the next two weeks.

Only steps away from jumping back into the thick of it, he breathed, in and out. *Take it easy, mate.* Sounds of the city assaulted his senses: car horns, a bus spitting exhaust fumes, a siren wailing in the distance. It was a loud city to be sure.

"Having second thoughts?" Jeremy Barnes said, standing next to him.

"What, and miss the chance to chastise you at every turn?"

"Enough, already," Cassie said, stepping next to Max.

He always knew when she was close by her scent: crisp and fresh, like mango.

"Could you help with the bags, Mr. Barnes?" Cassie said.

"My pleasure."

Max started up the stairs, irritated that she didn't ask him for help. No, Max was the broken one, the cripple. Then why the hell had they asked him to lead this project?

He stepped onto the landing and hesitated. "Is everyone here?"

"Mostly. You ready?" Barnes said.

"Why not?" He opened the door and stepped inside.

Cassie and Barnes shared a look behind him, he could feel it. Amazing how people thought since he was psychologically impaired that he missed things: awkward moments, tender moments. Since the bombing, Max had discovered that in some ways he could sense a lot more than the average man. Then again, maybe that was a symptom of going mad.

He made his way through the front hall while Barnes carried the bags up to the second floor. The thought of Barnes waiting on him gave Max perverse pleasure.

"Good morning," he said, entering the main room, head up, back straight, trying to downplay his disability. He'd always had a presence. No reason to think he'd lost that along with his mind.

"How's everyone?" He slipped off his leather jacket and tossed it to the desk. He turned to address the team.

"Hey, guv, bloody good to see you," Art McDonald said

with a firm handshake. He wore his usual burnt-orange suit and loud-patterned tie. The man lived for the seventies.

"Haven't changed your style of dress, I see," Max said.

"No, sir. You look fantastic. You're on the mend, still on holiday in the U.S.?"

"You bet."

That was his official line when he'd left SCI: after seventeen years of round-the-clock police work, Max was taking a long-deserved holiday in the U.S. He'd been too ashamed to admit the truth: he was running from his ghosts.

They shook hands and Art's grip calmed Max's racing heartbeat. Not nerves, he told himself, just the usual rush from starting a case.

"Bobby Finn's here too, guv."

"Hello, guv'nor," Bobby said, entering from the hallway. "It's an honor to be working with you again."

Ten years ago Max had convinced the angry teenager to trade his criminal ways for a career in law enforcement. Bobby would become a fine investigator one day, once he learned to rein in his emotions. Bobby shook Max's hand, his eyes expressing respect, maybe even awe.

Most of the boys Max had worked with at SCI held him in high regard. Max had solved cases that had baffled other investigators by making sense of clues that had been casually dismissed.

Max had the uncanny ability to step into the criminal's mind, to become the criminal and gain insight. Apparently he hadn't stepped far enough into C.K.'s world. Ah, well, that cock-up hadn't seemed to tarnish his rep with McDonald and Finn.

"You boys have come a long way," Max said.

"Wouldn't miss a chance like this, sir," McDonald said.

"Who's this, guv?" Bobby asked, nodding at Cassie.

"Cassie Clarke, Agents Finn and McDonald."

Bobby Finn leaned forward to shake her hand, a little too far forward.

"You with the Chicago PD?" McDonald said.

"No, I'm Mr. Templeton's assistant."

"No kidding?" Bobby smiled, a twinkle in his eye.

Great, he could tell Cassie was going to be a distraction for the boys. Why not? She distracted the hell out of Max most days.

Her crisp scent and sunny personality would breeze into his flat each morning, taunting him with what could never be. He'd never be romantically involved again. He would never saddle a woman he cared about with his disabilities.

"Can you assist us as well?" Bobby had always been a flirt.

"Okay, let's get to work." Max leaned toward her and whispered into Cassie's ear. "Maybe you should dress a little more conservatively tomorrow, yeah?"

"What's wrong with what I'm wearing?"

He glanced at her outfit: black jeans and a short-sleeved shirt, tight enough to show the curve of her breast.

What's wrong indeed. "Maybe you shouldn't have come."

Yet a part of him was relieved. She had a way of grounding him, calming him during his episodes. They never spoke of it. He couldn't admit defeat to a senseless mental disorder. Yet here, in a strange city, working a gruesome murder case, he appreciated her presence.

Careful. She's just an employee.

"I'm here to help you stay on track with the book, and assist you with the investigation," she said.

"I'm not paying you for the latter."

"No, Mr. Barnes is."

Barnes? Had he hired Cassie to be his personal spy, to report back on whether Max was working the case or falling apart? If he had such little faith in Max, why had he asked him to lead the team?

Max suddenly understood Barnes's motivation—guilt.

No matter. It would give Max the opportunity to redeem himself.

"I believe taking a paycheck from me and from Mr. Barnes is called double-dipping," he said to Cassie.

"I'm sure I'll earn every penny of it." She glanced up at him. "I'm sorry, I shouldn't have said it that way."

Why not? He deserved it. No doubt he was the nastiest boss she'd ever had.

"Look, you're in foreign territory," she said.

"I'm not completely helpless, Miss Clarke."

"I didn't say you were. It's just, well, I'm here to help."

And make a hefty sum off her regular salary plus Barnes's donation. Somehow that cocky bloke would come out smelling like a rose. He always did.

"Okay, people! Let's get started," he ordered.

Chairs shuffled, voices hushed. They settled down, but the room hummed with anticipation.

"I'm Max Templeton, former team leader of the Special Crime Initiative of Scotland Yard. You all know Jeremy Barnes," he said, trying to keep the distaste from his voice. "He's second in command. We've got an excellent team assembled—from Scotland Yard, Agents Bobby Finn and Art McDonald. They worked on C.K. cases in London."

"C.K.?" a female voice asked.

"Crimson Killer," Max said. "More on that later. Let's go around the room and get acquainted."

The female, Ruth Kreegan, forensic specialist for the county, introduced herself. Kreegan had been instrumental in catching the Soda Serial Killer, a case that had gone cold for more than a decade. She'd started her career in the military, then had gone into civilian service as a forensic scientist. Her husband was with the Chicago PD bomb unit. Barnes had initially solicited another expert, who was sidelined by a car accident. They were lucky that Kreegan could fill in at the last minute.

Former Chicago Police detective, Joe Spinelli introduced himself. Spinelli, late thirties, had taken early retirement to start his own detective agency. He'd been hired by the family of the first victim to investigate the young man's death. He had fifteen plus years with the Chicago PD, mostly in homicide. Spinelli's detective skills and local contacts would be a great asset.

For the next fourteen days, Max, Barnes, Art McDonald, Bobby Finn, Ruth Kreegan and Joe Spinelli would be the Blackwell Group.

"Hey, guv, what about—"

"That's another thing," Max cut off Bobby Finn. "We're all agents and will refer to each other as such. We work as a team, sharing any and all information, no matter how silly or insignificant. The team will only succeed if we work together. Got it?"

"Yes, sir," the group answered.

The door opened and closed with a crash. "Sorry I'm late."

A young man, maybe twenty-five, raced into the room and slid behind a desk. He wore a black baseball cap with a dog on the front, a navy blue T-shirt and jeans, topped off by a corduroy blazer.

"And you are?" Max said.

"Eddie Malone, freelance computer geek at your service. I would have been here an hour ago but traffic on the Dan Ryan was a killer."

A few of the boys chuckled.

"We don't need the details," Max said. "Be on time tomorrow. We've only got fourteen days."

"Yes, sir."

"Here's the gist of it—the Crimson Killer targets male victims, eighteen to twenty-two years old, well off by most people's standards."

"We're assuming C.K. is a man?" said forensics expert Kreegan.

"We are. The London victims were all healthy, strapping lads able to defend themselves," Max said. "The Chicago murders are the same, yeah?"

"Yes, sir," Barnes said. "Athletic young men, hardworking, both disappeared without notice."

"Let's review the London cases," Max started. "Each victim is kidnapped and held for two days before the body is found. He's been strangled with a crimson scarf, his lips painted with crimson lipstick, and a red tea bag is found on the body. We had a suspect, but not enough evidence to arrest him."

"The suspect supposedly died in a car accident, but no body was ever found," Barnes added. "The murders stopped. Until now."

"Did the killer contact the Chicago Police?" Max said.

"Yes, sir," Agent Spinelli answered. "A buddy of mine says they received a note before the first kid was kidnapped, but didn't think anything of it. They thought it was some crackpot."

"The note was poetry?"

"Yes, sir. After I got hired by the boy's father, I did some research and found similarities with the SCI case in London—red scarf, painted lips, red tea bag."

"Our killer likes leaving clues and stringing us along. That's his game," Max said. "Agent Barnes, you included information from the previous murders in everyone's folder, yeah?"

"Yes, sir."

"Good, this is how it goes—Agent Spinelli, follow up with local witnesses. Talk to anyone who saw the victims just before they disappeared. Talk to friends. Ask about daily routines, party habits, strange occurrences at work. Agent Kreegan, I need a rundown of everything found at the scene, even if it seems insignificant. Late Eddie?"

"Sir?"

"I need you to get into the victims' personal computers. Check their appointment calendars, e-mails, instant messages, that sort of thing."

"Do you think they knew the killer?" Agent Kreegan said.

"It's possible," Max said. "We have to work all the angles."

"Could it be a copycat?" Late Eddie asked.

"Unlikely. We kept the gory details out of the press and didn't call it a serial case right off. On the other hand, if this *is* a copycat, that will work in our favor. This murderer should follow C.K.'s pattern so we'll know what's coming. Other questions?"

"No, sir," was the collective answer.

"Good. I picked this building because of its central

location. It's easy to get to if you're taking public transport from the suburbs, which I hear is very dependable." He paused and glanced at Late Eddie. A couple of the boys chuckled at the hint.

"Also, there's plenty of room for all of us. I know some of you have families and won't be spending the night. Barnes and I will be here twenty-four/seven. I'm assuming Agents McDonald and Finn will be camping out?"

"Yes, sir," McDonald said.

"And me," Cassie added.

"My assistant, Cassie Clarke," Max introduced. "She'll be assisting me with paperwork and incidentals. All right, let's get started. Agent Finn, tag along with Spinelli for interviews. Listen closely to witnesses and family. Something might set off a red flag, something you heard in the previous investigation that we didn't think significant."

"And me, guv?" Art McDonald said.

"Interview the parents of the second victim, ask about the boy's mood lately, marks in school, new friends, you know the drill."

"Yes, sir."

"If C.K. follows the pattern, we'll have exactly two days after we receive the next poem to stop him from killing again. Agent Barnes, I need you to walk through the latest crime scene with me."

"Gladly, sir."

"Cassie will be with us. Oh, and Late Eddie, contact someone in the FBI and see if they've recorded any similar crimes in the past year. Maybe these aren't his first two victims. That's it, then. We'll check in at four-thirty."

The group broke up and he motioned to Barnes. "They have everything they need?"

"It's all set up, sir."

"Good work."

"What, sir?" Barnes said.

"Don't expect me to repeat it."

"Of course not, sir," Barnes said. "Would you like to visit the crime scene now?"

"Give me a minute."

"Yes, sir."

The room buzzed with personal introductions and conversation. With a hand gripping his cane, Max aimed for the hallway, welcoming a few of the team members along the way. He made it to the bathroom, locked the door and turned on the faucet.

Take a deep breath. Count your heartbeats. One, two, three, four. You made it like a pro.

He splashed cool water on his face and stared at the reflection in the mirror. He could do this. Hell, he'd just *done* this. They all looked to him, expected him to lead this investigation and catch C.K. before he killed his next victim. They didn't care about Max's limp or random spells that left him breathless.

With a quick swipe of a towel, he dried his face and

hands. He took another deep breath and started down the hall in search of Barnes.

"Mr. Templeton?" Cassie called.

She came up beside Max, the top of her blond head barely reaching his chin. "Mr. Barnes said for us to wait by the front door."

They ambled to the front and he tugged at his tie. "So, how did I do?"

"What?"

"In the briefing, how did I do?"

She opened her mouth, then closed it.

"That bad?" he said. "I must have really lost my touch."

She gripped his arm and the warmth shot straight to his heart. Pathetic.

"You were very commanding," she said.

"And you want a raise."

"No, I mean it. It's just, you never seemed to need reassurance before. It's a new look for you."

"Ah, don't worry. I'll be back to my old self again soon."

"Too bad," she whispered.

"What?"

"Ready?" Barnes said, coming up behind them.

Great, how much of that had Barnes heard?

"Let's go." Max took a step toward the door. A high-pitched squeak pinched his eardrums. God, no, not another spell. He tapped at his temple with the heel of his palm.

"You okay?" Barnes asked.

Max shook it off and opened the door. "Never better," he said, stepping into the Chicago sunshine.

CASSIE WATCHED the men talk, squat, take a few steps one way and a few steps the other, on the sand at the Northside Beach. This city was a beautiful place, when visiting.

Distant memories whispered to her: a mother and three girls playing in the sand, building castles and chasing waves.

"You still with us?" Max said.

"Yes, Mr. Templeton, I'm sorry. I got caught up in this perfect day." She walked up to the men.

"A perfect day for finding a killer, you mean."

He would bring her back down to earth, robbing her of the simplest pleasure: a peaceful moment at the beach. That's what Mr. Templeton did: focused on the darkness and shut out the light.

Some days she wondered why she'd hung around this long. Then she'd find him screaming in his sleep, and she knew why.

Of course, she'd initially taken the job because no one else at her temp agency wanted the assignment. Two of the girls had already quit due to his demanding nature and high expectations. Not only did he expect them to do computer work, but occasionally he'd ask his assistant to pick up groceries and run errands. The first two girls were offended by the request, but Cassie didn't mind. Money was money, and she was getting paid a decent wage for a part-time job, which afforded her time to volunteer at the women's shelter.

"It doesn't add up," Mr. Barnes said. "If the boy was killed here, why didn't anyone see or hear anything? If the body was dumped, it would have taken quite a bit of time to stage it."

"Which means?" Mr. Templeton said.

"I haven't a clue."

"Which is why I was your boss."

Max smiled, thoroughly enjoying taunting Mr. Barnes.

"Nice guy," Cassie said in sympathy with Mr. Barnes.

"Well, thank you, Miss Clarke." Mr. Templeton brushed sand from his fingers. "One thing I didn't lose in the bombing is my hearing. Might want to keep that in mind next time you're going to talk behind my back in my presence."

"I was kidding. Sorry, sir."

"Nothing to be sorry for. I'm an ogre. I know it."

"And such an intuitive man," Barnes added.

Mr. Templeton almost smiled, but the smile faded and his jaw clenched tight.

She dreaded his silence more than his angry temperament. It meant he was having one of his episodes, like a seizure, but not. It was like something lit up his brain, and he tried desperately to focus the many pieces into a clear picture.

Cassie touched his arm to ground him. That's about all

she could do. She felt helpless. After it passed, as always, they would both pretend nothing had happened. They'd never talk about it; he'd never formally thanked her.

But she'd seen appreciation in his eyes, if only for a few seconds. She knew that vulnerability was appalling to a man like Max Templeton.

"Are you okay?" Barnes asked.

"Give him a minute," Cassie said. "He'll be fine."

Jeremy hadn't had a second thought about bringing Max into this case, until now. Was he in a trance? Was this a post-traumatic stress attack of some sort?

Jeremy remembered when Max had tried returning to SCI after the bombing. On the third day Jeremy had found him at his desk breathing as if he'd run a marathon. Jeremy had guessed Max was suffering from post-traumatic stress syndrome. And who wouldn't be after being nearly blown to bits?

A few days later Max had taken his leave of absence and guilt had torn Jeremy apart. It should have been Jeremy at King's Cross Station that day. Instead, he was stuck in traffic at Heathrow. He'd never forgiven himself for that.

Nor had Max. Well, for that and for being healthy, active and taking Max's job as the new team leader at SCI. Max would malign Jeremy to his own grandmother if given the chance, yet loyalty held Jeremy firm to Max's side. He cared about the talented, genius bastard. A fact he'd never openly admit. Nor would he ever admit how hard he'd fought to get Max the lead position for the Blackwell Group.

"I'm okay." Max wavered on his cane; it seemed a little wonky on the unsteady sand.

Cassie held on to his arm. "You're not used to sand, sir."

"Or the heat," Max said.

It was a mild fall day in Chicago, maybe seventy degrees. Jeremy considered what to say next. Was this too much for Max? He didn't want to put the man at risk.

"Barnes?" Max said.

"Sir?"

"I need to see the last victim's belongings."

"Yes, sir."

"Immediately."

Chapter Three

Max hated the dizziness and disorientation. Maybe it was time to see another specialist. A neurologist, perhaps? He'd been avoiding doctors for fear they'd only give him worse news.

Can't get much worse, mate.

Sure it could. He could lose his trusty assistant, the girl who held him up and wasn't scared off by his freakish episodes. He needed her more than he wanted to admit, and the thought of needing someone that much drove him mad.

Max and Cassie waited for Barnes, who was getting evidence from Spinelli. Spinelli relied on his connection with the Chicago PD to get the team a brief look at the evidence, which is why they waited here, at a coffee shop close to property storage.

Tapping his fingers on the table's cool surface, he thought about the killer's games, and the way he'd taunted Max during the London investigation. C.K. had sent Max running in circles.

"Are you nervous?" Cassie asked.

Hell, he'd forgotten she was with him.

"Not nervous, why?" he said.

"Your fingers. You're tapping them like a musician."

He leaned back and crossed his arms over his chest. This girl should be the detective.

"You kept a steady beat with your fingertips," she said. "Do you play an instrument?"

The door opened and in walked Barnes with a brown paper bag.

Saved by Barnes. Ironic. The last thing Max wanted was to share intimate secrets with Cassie. Secrets about sneaking into Tula's Jazz Club after hours to hear the boys jam. Anything to avoid lying awake and realizing his failures, berating himself for not catching C.K.

And berating himself for being unable to help innocent victims of the bombing because he'd been pinned by the wreckage.

Barnes pulled up a chair. "These are from the victims. I have to get it back to Spinelli in thirty minutes."

Max opened the bag and inspected the contents.

"The first victim was Michael Cunningham," Jeremy started. "Age twenty, student at Jamison College, actually both victims were students at Jamison. Cunningham was from a wealthy family in Pennsylvania. He was studying business, working part-time at a bookstore."

Max focused on each item encased in plastic wrap: a scarf, tea bag and key chain.

"Did Chicago Police trace the scarf?" Max said.

"Not sure, sir."

"Have Spinelli find out."

"Yes, sir."

"Red tea, Sterling Brand. Cassie, make a note to find out if this is a popular brand overseas as well as in the States."

"Sure," she said, opening her steno pad. He hoped she wouldn't mind doing investigative work. Researching tea seemed a safe enough assignment.

He picked up a wallet, then a house key and a lighter.

"He smoked?"

Barnes flipped a few pages in his notebook. "There's no record of that, sir."

Interesting. "Cassie, jot a few things down for me, will you?"

"Sure."

Max sifted through the evidence. "Loose change, credit cards, a student ID and video store gift card." He looked at Barnes. "Did the boy drive?"

Barnes flipped a few pages in his notebook. "Yes, he owned a Ford Escort."

"There's no driver's license here." He nodded to Cassie to write that down.

The killer took his license? C.K. had never done that before.

"No cash," Max said. "What do you make of this?" He slid the keychain across the table toward Barnes.

"Looks like a fraternity symbol," he said. "Both victims were members of Sigma Delta Upsilon."

Could it be a cover-up for a fraternity hazing gone wrong? *Anything was possible*—the motto that had helped Max solve impossible cases at SCI.

Max inspected an official-looking letter from the college. "Looks like a progress report. The boy wasn't doing well."

"Which could account for his late-night walkabout on the beach?" Barnes offered.

"I'm not making that jump." He turned the progress report over and read the scribblings. "'Screw them all… They'll all pay… That bitch will die.'"

Cassie didn't look up from her note-taking. He could tell by the way she nibbled at her lower lip that the violent nature of the words bothered her.

He shouldn't have brought her into this. He should have shelved his anxiety and taken his chances with the post-trauma attacks. Once Cassie knew what Max excelled at, that he loved this kind of gruesome work, she'd find another cripple to care for, one in a more palatable line of work.

"Agent Barnes, interview his college advisor, female professors, former girlfriends. See if he's violent towards women, or if he's a lot of talk."

"Respectfully, sir, I don't see how—"

"It's the big picture, Barnes. You know the artist, Seurat? Up close it's all dots. It's not until you step back and take in every stroke of the brush touching the canvas that you make out the complete image."

"Yes, sir."

"How about the second victim?" Max asked.

"Peter Stanton from Michigan," Barnes said. "Upper-crust family, father is a General Motors executive. Pre-med student."

Max sifted through the items. "Similar scarf, same tea bag. Contents of wallet—credit cards, twenty-dollar bill, library card, transit card, no driver's license. Same fraternity keychain." He fingered an odd-looking coin. "Hello, what's this?"

"Looks like a foreign coin," Cassie offered.

Max inspected the copper coin, dulled by age.

"I've also got some photographs," Barnes said, pulling pictures of the crime scenes out of an envelope.

Cassie glanced at the photos, then snapped her attention to her notepad. Max reviewed the photos and passed them back. Had the brutal nature of the crimes upset her?

"Cassie?" he said.

She hesitated at first and glanced at him. "Sorry, I was distracted."

By what, he wondered? "Let's get some lunch. Barnes, take these back to Spinelli and we'll meet you at the command center."

"Yes, sir." He packed up and left the coffee shop.

Cassie continued to study her notepad.

"Let's go," Max led her to the door. She opened the door for him, but he motioned for her to walk through first. He was still a gentleman, although some days he might not act like it.

"When was the last time you saw a doctor?" she said.

"I don't need a doctor." He gripped his cane and aimed for the street corner.

She looked up at him. "They're coming out with new drugs all the time for conditions like yours."

"You mean something to make me all better? A miracle drug to stop the nightmares?" He ripped his gaze from hers and studied a group of tourists ahead of them. "Maybe they've even got something to help me type. Then I wouldn't need you, would I?"

Inside he panicked. She was much more than a secretary. She was his only contact with the outside world. His condition created a kind of isolation he wouldn't choose for his worst enemy. Even Barnes.

"I only brought it up because I know how much you hate it," she said.

Out of the corner of his eye, he could tell she still looked at him.

"The episodes, I mean," she said.

"I know what you meant."

They walked in silence, the strain of their conversation weighing heavy in his chest. She wanted to help, but he didn't want to be anyone's pet project, especially not hers.

What's that about, mate?

Nothing, absolutely nothing. He was rattled by the odd evidence of the case. He snapped his attention to Cassie.

"The photographs, the descriptions of the crimes, it's only going to get worse," he said. "This case might be too gruesome for a girl like yourself. It's totally understandable if you want out."

"No, I'm okay."

The forced sound of her voice spoke otherwise. Honesty from the people closest to him was critical. He'd have to explain that to her over lunch.

CASSIE ACCOMPANIED her employer to the corner, puzzling over his concern. He'd never seemed to care about her needs before. He mostly barked orders or criticized the way she made coffee. She didn't take it personally. She knew he wasn't mad at her, but at his own vulnerability.

It troubled her that he thought a few graphic photographs would make her quit working for him. Obviously he didn't think her tough enough to deal with the ugly details of a murder case.

Don't go there, girl. He doesn't know you well enough to make that jump.

Maybe leaving his oppressive apartment had shaken the porcupine-like prickles from his skin. Could there really be a compassionate man living inside that incredible body? Now *there* was a place she couldn't go, not if she wanted to keep this job.

This was the first truly flexible, well-paying job she'd had since the move to Seattle. The others had either paid minimum wage, or demanded forty-plus hours a week. She needed some of those hours for herself, and for the girls at the shelter. With her salary from Max and the bonus offered by Mr. Barnes she'd finally found a little financial stability.

To think Karl had said she was only good for blow jobs and housekeeping.

Karl. She hadn't thought about that monster in a while. She had to admit, putting up with his abuse had hardened her against rude people…like Max.

But she knew grief fueled Max's anger. In his mind, the bombing had robbed him of his identity and maybe even his soul as sure as a pickpocket snatching a wallet from a tourist.

What a shame. He might struggle with post-traumatic stress and a hip injury that caused him to depend on a cane, but he was very much a healthy, intelligent man. His description of Seurat's work surprised her. A hard-ass like Max actually appreciating fine art? Amazing. His body was in prime form as well. Even with the cane he moved with utter confidence. She envied that.

"There's one," he said, waving a cab. He wobbled slightly.

"Are you okay?" She knew he didn't get out much back home. Were all the people and commotion stressing him out?

"I'm fine," he said, his voice laced with irritation.

She guessed he didn't want to be reminded of his injury, of his weakness.

"I'd like to review the case files at lunch," he said.

A cab pulled to the curb.

"There's a pub around the corner from the command center. We'll eat and you can tell me what's really troubling you." He smiled and opened the door for her.

Great, a heart-to-heart with Max Templeton, intuitive detective, insightful male and demanding boss. She couldn't climb out the other side of the cab and send it on its way, could she?

SHE WAS KEEPING something from him; he could feel it in his bones. Max didn't need another mystery element to this case.

Like the mystery of the missing driver's license? If the killer had taken it, that meant they weren't dealing with their old friend from London. Or it meant C.K. had changed his M.O. Not good. Being able to anticipate his next move would help keep the next victim alive. If C.K. had switched tactics it would be yet another challenge.

And Max's brain was already struggling with its own set of challenges, madness topping the list.

He wrapped his hand around his beer glass and listened to the sounds of the lunch crowd: a baseball game on the telly, intermittent laughter and idle chatter.

This case, chasing after C.K., brought him back to

life a bit. It felt good to be needed and respected, but it would all crumble at his feet if he couldn't trust the people around him.

"Cassie?"

"Yes?"

"We need to get things on the table."

"I've got the folders right here. Which do you need?"

"Not those things. I need to know why you're really here." There, he'd said it. There had to be something that had made her come all the way to Chicago besides a financial incentive from Barnes.

"It's my job. Mr. Barnes made it worth my while," she teased.

"There's more to it."

"Hey, I'm an employee, not your psych patient."

"I don't want you to bare your soul to me." On the other hand, maybe he did. "But here it is." He leaned back in the booth and crossed his arms over his chest, studying her petite form as she fidgeted across the table from him. "I've got plenty of puzzles filling my brain. Why has C.K. resurfaced in Chicago? Is it really C.K. or a copycat? Why did Barnes ask me to lead the team? The list goes on. You can't be one of those puzzles. I need to trust you completely. I need to know that everything you do, you do with my best interest in mind. I can't feel that kind of trust if you keep things from me."

"What makes you think I'm keeping something from you?"

"I just know. You're not yourself."

"Right." She chuckled. "Not my usual flaky self these days?"

"I never thought of you as flaky, but rather, energetic, cheerful."

"And that must drive you nuts."

"Stop avoiding the question," he said. "What is it? Is the thought of a serial killer getting to you?"

She didn't answer. He waited, listened to the man at the table next to them complain to his lunch companion about his job.

"I used to live here," she admitted.

"Why did you move?"

"Bad marriage."

He realized how little he knew about her. "How long ago?"

"I lived here most of my life," she said. "I moved to Seattle a year and a half ago. I thought coming back would help me find completion."

"I'm sorry," he paused, "about the marriage."

"Don't be. It made me tough."

"Maybe not as tough as you think."

"What's that supposed to mean?"

He hesitated.

"What?" she pushed.

"I'm not sure I'm comfortable making you look at gruesome photographs and take notes about murder details."

"You don't think I can handle it? Listen, I'm here to help you with this investigation any way I can. Don't coddle me, Mr. Templeton, or I'll have to quit."

He'd hit a nerve. She wanted everyone to think of her as strong and confident. Who was Max to challenge her wishes?

"It's a deal. No coddling," he said. "Is there anything else I need to know about you?"

"What, like my bra size?" she joked.

He guessed that was her way of telling him to back off. He had to respect her space. Deep down he knew she wasn't a personal threat.

"Okay, here is how it will go," he said. "In order to do my job, I must trust you completely. In order to do that, I need to know you won't share information with Agent Barnes or anyone else on the team without my permission."

"You don't trust Jeremy?" she said, with an innocent blink of blue eyes.

"Jeremy?" he repeated. Barnes must have already charmed her if she was referring to him by his first name. She rarely called Max by his.

"I don't trust Agent Barnes," he continued. "We have a history. Can you respect my wishes?"

"Yes, sir."

A waitress slid a plate in front of Max and the smell of fried food awakened his taste buds. They didn't make fish and chips like back home, but he kept hoping he'd find a pub that came close.

"Thank you," Cassie said to the waitress.

Max nodded his thanks, plucked a chip from the plate and popped it into his mouth.

"May I ask a question?" she said.

"Sure." He reached for his knife and fork.

"What happened to you?"

"I'm sorry?" He stabbed a piece of fish with his fork.

"What happened that made you…like this?"

"You mean the bombing that ruined my life? Ah, that's simple. It's called payback."

"Excuse me?"

"I was where I shouldn't have been, in time to be the victim of a terrorist bombing. I didn't get shot on duty, or crack up in a car thanks to one too many pints. I got struck down at random as punishment for being a selfish bastard."

"I'm sure that isn't the case."

"You didn't know me then. Wasn't a charmer like I am now," he said with a smile. "Even drove my fiancée away."

"Your fiancée?" she said, amazement in her voice.

"Yep, the reason I moved to Seattle—Lydia Drake."

Just before she'd abandoned him, Lydia claimed it was Max's self-pity that had ruined their relationship. He knew the truth: she didn't want to be saddled to a cripple whose terrifying nightmares haunted him day and night.

"She had this great career opportunity in Seattle and I wasn't doing anything important other than having multiple surgeries on my hip, so she brought me along," Max said. "Set me up with doctors, enrolled me in physical therapy."

"Sounds like she loved you very much."

"She brought me to the States to be her sex toy."

Cassie choked on her drink.

"What, the truth shocks you?" He leaned forward and spoke low. "Lydia said, 'Come to Seattle, we'll spend weekends on the coast and tour Victoria Island. The perfect place for an extended holiday.' Instead, she stuck me in the flat and worked ten-hour days, six days a week. I was expected to have dinner ready at seven and fulfill her sexual needs at nine-thirty. If that offends your sensibilities then you're too fragile for this kind of work. I'll buy you a plane ticket and send you back to Seattle tomorrow morning."

"And you'll be safe," she said.

"Safe?" He sat back. "From what?"

"From being honest with yourself. If you hide out in your apartment you'll be safe from learning to cope with your condition. I've got news for you—you can hide but it doesn't go away. You want to send me back so you'll be safe from the one person who won't let you get away with this self-destructive garbage."

"You think I'm afraid of you?"

"Desperately, because I want to help you. I can bring you back to life and the thought terrifies you."

"Is that what you're about? Saving lost causes?" He

narrowed his eyes. "I've heard about women like you. Was your husband a lost cause? Needed a little shot of self-confidence and you were there shaking your pom-poms and making it all better?" He tasted the bitter words on his tongue, but he couldn't stop. "What happened, did he outgrow his little cheerleader? Send you packing because he'd found someone better?"

"Not exactly," she said, her voice soft, but still firm. "He put me in the hospital."

"Blast," he muttered. He should be struck down by lightning for twisting that knife through this sweet girl's heart. "I'm sorry."

"Be sorry for yourself, not me. I've healed. You haven't."

"I never will. It's not like I'll wake up one day and be my old self again."

"You talk like you're the only one who's had to deal with serious crap," she said in a raised voice. "My ex-husband broke my back, put me in the hospital for two months and tracked me down at my sister's when I got out. I had to abandon my family and friends in Chicago so I could get away from him and not put them in danger. The first six months in Seattle were hell, and my body still aches some days, thanks to him, but I don't go around moaning about it."

Cassie saw the line, crossed it and kept on running. She couldn't help herself. She'd developed a new kind of strength where self-pity was concerned. Strength she had used to encourage the girls at the shelter to leave abusive situations. She was their champion, their inspiration. It made her feel as though the years spent with Karl weren't wasted.

Yet the investigator sitting across from her wasn't an abused wife on the run. He was a man whose life had been stripped from him at random. He deserved a little compassion.

"I shouldn't have spoken to you like that," she said, clutching her locket. An old, comforting habit.

"Actually, it's entirely refreshing to see another side of my little blond assistant." He smiled.

He looked so handsome when he smiled, his green eyes lighting up, his face looking softer, more touchable than when he scowled. She suddenly realized it had been a very long time since she'd been attracted to a man, and even longer since she'd wanted to touch one.

"I was being an ass," he said. "I deserved a good thrashing." He chomped on a piece of fish.

"As long as we're being honest," she hesitated, "I've got a suggestion about your appearance."

"What, did I spill?" He glanced at his shirt.

"No, but you could use a shave."

He rubbed his full beard. "I think it suits me."

"You look like a bum."

"Appearances can be deceiving. First rule of investigative work."

"Yeah, well, you wouldn't have to worry about getting food caught in your beard if you shaved it off."

A piece of fish breading clung to the corner of his mouth. She reached out with her napkin to brush it away.

He grabbed her wrist as if the physical contact wounded him. It was such a gentle touch for such a powerful man.

She waited, searching his green eyes. She read only pain.

He let go of her wrist and pulled back so quickly he knocked over his drink.

"Bollocks," he muttered, slipping out from the booth to avoid the dripping beer. "Miss?" He motioned for the waitress.

His cell phone rang. He pulled it from his suit jacket and handed it to Cassie, while he continued to dab the beer from his pants.

"This is Cassie," she said.

Max studied her expression.

"It's Jeremy. We received a note. You'd better get back to the command center."

"We'll be right there." She snapped the phone shut.

"Another poem," Max said, matter-of-factly.

"How did you know?" she asked.

"Bloody hell."

THEY WORKED so hard, the fools. They swarmed the note like ants on a morsel of cake. Led by one big, pompous ant.

But they weren't smart enough. Not to save these bastards. They deserved to die. Why couldn't they accept that?

Ah, let them run in circles, back to where they started. And everything would be as it should. Work hard, little ants. In two weeks the boys would all be dead. It will finally be over.

Chapter Four

Jeremy stood in the doorway and watched Max pace the small den in the back of the house. Cassie reread the note that had been dropped off at police headquarters, addressed to Max. Cassie and Max had been back here for half an hour while the rest of the team waited for Max's directive.

Max was obsessing over this one, that was for certain, but he was no good to them in a highly emotional state. Emotions muddled things, clouded an investigator's perspective. Jeremy believed in facts and process, in not letting the humanity of a case get to him.

"Again," Max said.

The girl cleared her throat. *"'A cruel trick lights my wick/ A quick game isn't the same/ Lies, betrayal and torture/ Giving up and giving in/ You will be struck down, Inspector. Again.'"*

Silence blanketed the room. The reference to Max was chilling. C.K. had never directly challenged him before. The murderer seemed to be taunting Max, daring him to try and catch the scoundrel who had killed four young men in London and two in Chicago.

Max tapped his fingers against the brass handle of his cane.

"Max?" Jeremy interrupted.

He snapped his attention to Jeremy. The intensity of his eyes nearly made Jeremy step back.

"I'm sorry, Agent Templeton," Jeremy corrected. "They're waiting for a directive, sir."

Jeremy didn't want Max to appear weak or indecisive. Finn and McDonald were familiar with his skill at solving cases, but he still had to prove himself to the rest of the team.

"I'll be right in," Max said.

"Yes, sir." Jeremy headed down the hallway to the front room. "Agent Templeton is coming straight away," he said. "Everyone be ready with an update."

Bobby Finn approached. "Is he okay, guv?"

Good man, Bobby. Max had taken him under his wing and the boy would always keep a look out for his mentor.

"He's fine." Jeremy turned to the group. "What have we got so far?"

"No prints on the note," Agent Kreegan said from her desk. "Nothing unusual about the printing or the paper used. It could be purchased at any office supply store."

"How about theories on a victim connection?"

Jeremy crossed his arms over his chest, shoving back his frustration.

"The victims' fraternity seems to be the only connection," Spinelli said. "It's a typical frat house with your usual keggers, mixers, stuff like that."

"Any personal connection between the two men? Were they friends?"

"Not really," Spinelli said.

"Anything strange happen to them before their deaths? Threats, phone calls?"

"Not that anyone mentioned, sir." Spinelli paged through his small notebook. "Cunningham was hardworking, a bit of a hot-head, struggled with schoolwork. The other one, Peter Stanton, was a party boy. One of the kids said he wasn't sure if Stanton would be back next semester. Thought he might flunk out."

"Were they in the same classes, extracurricular activities?"

"No, guv," Bobby offered. "They lived in the same fraternity house. That was the only connection."

"Who received the note?"

"It was dropped off at division headquarters on the north side." Spinelli glanced up at Jeremy. "I can't help but wonder if this has less to do with the victims and more to do with our boss. Considering the last line of the note, it seems pretty personal."

"They're all personal." Max strode into the room,

aiming for the front desk. He had to get it under control, keep a lid on the anger simmering in his chest.

"I'll take it from here, Agent Barnes." Max scanned his team. "The sooner we solidify a connection between the victims the closer we'll be to narrowing down suspects. The good news is," he paused, "this isn't like the rest of the poems. This one's about me. If the killer was setting the clock for his next murder, he would have told us with great fanfare."

"You think he's messing with us?" Spinelli said.

"That's exactly what he's doing," Max confirmed. "Stringing us along, sending us love notes. Waiting to see what we'll do next."

"You think he's in the area, guv?" Bobby Finn asked.

"In the area and most likely watching us."

"But why play games?" Eddie asked. "Why not cut to the chase and take his next victim?"

"Because the games are a turn-on," Art said. "Sorry to interrupt, guv."

"Agent McDonald is right," Max agreed. "This is the beginning of a very twisted game. The locals didn't know how to play, so C.K.'s pulling out all his tricks for us. Let's not get distracted. Focus on the case. The connection is the fraternity. Spinelli, interview anyone who stepped foot into the house in the last month—college girls looking for a good time, the cleaners, pest control, anyone. Ask the president about any odd circumstances, vandalism or threats. Agent McDonald, scan police reports of missing persons, male, eighteen to twenty-two years of age, and I mean scan with a magnifying glass. We can't risk that C.K.'s got another victim on hold."

That's it, keep it moving. Don't pause to take a breath. Don't let them see your panic.

You will be struck down, Inspector. Again.

This one *was* different. The killer was after Max.

"Late Eddie, I need that report on the victims' e-mails, especially incoming," Max said.

"Yes, sir."

"Next, who completed interviews with parents?"

"I've got information about the first boy's parents," Spinelli said.

"And I spoke briefly with the Stantons this morning, guv," Art offered.

"I need to see them."

"Sir, I found an interesting e-mail," Late Eddie offered.

"Read it out loud."

"It's a link to a *Tribune* article dated two months ago," Eddie started. "The headline reads, Sigma Delta Upsilon Receives Montgomery Grant for Community Service."

"All right, then. We've got a house of upstanding citizens stalked by a cold-blooded killer who likes to dominate, manipulate and control. Did I miss anything?"

"We're probably looking at a male, middle-aged, a loner," Agent Kreegan said.

Although he didn't expect a profile from a forensic scientist, she was right. It sounded a lot like their

London suspect. Max paced to the window and took a deep breath. No, something didn't feel right.

"We're not seeing something here." He turned to his team. "Something crucial."

"Like what, guv?" Bobby asked.

"If I knew I'd be in a whole lot better mood, wouldn't I?"

The room fell silent. Max had better watch it. It did him no good to take out his frustrations on the team. And he sure as hell didn't want to look like a right nutter who couldn't control his temper.

A man who couldn't keep it together.

"Agent Kreegan? Get me something off that note."

"Yes, sir."

"Barnes, make an appointment with the fraternity president," Max said. "That's it. Get to work."

Why was C.K. making this personal? He'd never taunted Max like this before.

"Can I get you anything, sir?" Barnes asked, concern lacing his voice.

Pity from Barnes nauseated Max.

"Where's Cassie?" Max said.

"I think she's in the back making a call."

"Get her, will you? I'll need you, Finn and Cassie to accompany me to district headquarters. I want to canvass the area, check security tapes. See if we can drum up leads as to who dropped off the note."

"Of course, sir."

Barnes disappeared and Max turned to glance out the front window of the command center. A blur of movement caught his eye: leaves being tossed about from the fall wind. Which was how he felt right now, tossed about, unable to get hold of anything.

"Sir?" Agent Kreegan said. "The notes you received during the London murders, were they printed on fancy paper?"

"Not particularly. Why?"

"Because this one was printed on parchment with little specks of red, pink and orange. Does it mean anything to you, sir?"

His blood chilled. Could C.K. have already taken his next victim and used the boy's blood to decorate the notepaper?

"Cassie!" he called.

"Yes, sir?" She strode into the room.

"The note, where is it?"

"I've got it," Barnes said, standing beside her.

"Give it to Agent Kreegan." He turned to her. "Test every speck for DNA. Results go directly to McDonald. He'll be working the missing-persons angle."

"Yes, sir." She grabbed a briefcase from her chair and left.

"My God," Cassie whispered. "You think that was blood on the note?"

"I doubt it," Max said. "Barnes, get her a glass of water, will you?"

"I'm fine," she said.

He heard the tremor in her voice.

"All the same." Barnes touched Cassie's shoulder and led her into the hallway toward the kitchen.

Max squeezed the brass handle of his cane. Did no good to be furious with Barnes for following an order. Only, Max didn't remember telling him to touch the girl.

She'd turned white at the suggestion of blood spatters on the note. How was Max going to do his job effectively *and* look out for her tender sensitivities at the same time?

Focus.

Max went to McDonald's desk. "I've got Agent Kreegan working on a lead. If she gets a blood type, see if it matches with any suspected missing boys."

"Wish we could get access to the FBI missing persons database," McDonald said.

"I've worked with the FBI. I can get us in, sir," Late Eddie offered. "Although, that would probably mean breaking twenty-seven different federal laws."

Max leaned over his desk. "Being a part of Blackwell means bending the rules to get results. This isn't a government agency. We do whatever it takes."

"Is that a direct order, sir?" Eddie said, with a twinkle in his eye.

"Yes, it is." He glanced across the room. "Agent Finn?"

"Yeah, guv?" Bobby walked over to Max.

"You're riding with us. Bring a car around, will you?"

"Right away, guv."

Max glanced at the doorway in time to see Cassie smile at something Barnes said. Her smile was innocent, yet charming, and Max was jealous that Barnes had put it there.

Perfect. Not only was Max a target of a serial killer's attention, but he also had to cope with rusty investigative skills, a strange mental disorder and now...jealousy.

What should he care if Barnes made her laugh, or even took her out and showed her a good time? She deserved a good time, something she was definitely not getting from Max.

Barnes leaned a little closer, whispered something, and she smiled.

Clenching his jaw, Max limped up between them trying to look unaffected by their flirtation.

"Bobby's bringing a car around," he said. "Cassie and I will sit in the back."

"Why, thank you, sir," Barnes said.

Was that a mocking grin on his face?

"Let's go," Max said. It was going to be a long afternoon.

IF SHE DIDN'T KNOW better, she'd think Max was jealous. Ridiculous, Cassie thought, following him to a liquor store around the corner from police headquarters.

He stopped and glared over his shoulder. "Stay here."

Taking a step back, she crossed her arms over her chest. Wow, the first two words he'd spoken since they'd left the command center: two emotionless words equaling an order.

As he disappeared into the store, she leaned up against the building. If it wasn't jealousy, then what? Was his hip bothering him more than usual, but he wouldn't admit it? He was determined not to show any weakness. He'd survived a deadly blast. It wasn't his fault he'd been injured. It wasn't exactly a personal weakness like being conceited or nasty.

No, he chose to be bossy, hardheaded and rude.

She thought they'd cleared the air during lunch: Cassie spilling her guts about Karl, Max telling her point-blank that he needed to trust her without reservation.

He sure wasn't acting like he trusted her. Sheesh, he acted as though he didn't even like her all that much.

She watched Jeremy and Bobby make their way down the other side of the street. They were asking business owners if they'd seen a man resembling the one who had dropped off the note. Thanks to Agent Spinelli's connections, he'd gotten a good description from a police lieutenant.

She watched Jeremy shake hands with a business-man. Jeremy was rather attractive, tall and lean, with a reserved nature and wry sense of humor. He seemed like a nice enough guy, a proper gentleman, but not her type.

No, she'd been conditioned to be drawn to the rough guys, hard-asses, maybe a little mean. Which is why she wasn't getting involved anytime soon. She wouldn't risk her own bad judgment. It would surely land her in a mess of chaos and pain. And it would be a frigid day in hell before she'd put herself in the position of depending on a man again, giving him that kind of power.

She guessed Max's ex-fiancée had depended on him before the accident. Cassie imagined that after the bombing, he'd pushed her away because he felt weak and helpless.

Cassie didn't see him that way at all. Withdrawn, sure, but definitely not weak.

Turning back to the street, she glanced at pedestrians who marched down the sidewalk toward their various jobs, appointments and lunches. She hoped that Max would stop hiding in his apartment and come out into the world on his own. In some respects, he was a lot like the women she worked with at the shelter: wounded, scared and distrustful. These were challenging emotions for a woman, they must be brutal for a typical man. Although, she wouldn't know a typical man if he walked up and kissed her on the cheek.

"Enough," she muttered, shaking off the self-condemnation.

Jeremy glanced in her direction and smiled. She smiled back, appreciating the friendly gesture.

"What is it with you two?"

She jumped at the sound of Max's voice and glanced up into his hard, green eyes.

"What, so absorbed in your fantasy about Agent Barnes that you didn't even hear me hobble up beside you?" Max said.

It was a rude remark. But at least he was talking to her.

Girl, you've got to learn some new tricks.

She narrowed her eyes, winding up for a good comeback. But before she could utter a word, he shook his head and walked away. Walked, not hobbled. He never hobbled. Why was he determined to berate himself for needing the cane? Was it *that* horrible to be dependent on something?

Yes, she thought, for Max Templeton, it was appalling.

"Hey, wait up!" she called after him.

Jeremy waved them over. Apparently they had found a lead. Max practically sprinted through traffic to get away from her.

Good grief, Cassie! He wants to find a killer. This isn't about him getting away from you.

Or was it?

She danced through traffic and caught up to him. Max, Jeremy and Bobby were deep in conversation. "She said a man fitting the description of the suspect visits her espresso stand Monday through Thursday afternoons, around four," Jeremy said.

"She's sure it's him?"

"Pretty sure, guv," Bobby said. "Gray hooded sweatshirt, a pierced eyebrow, she thinks Hispanic."

"He can't be our killer," Jeremy said.

"Maybe not, but he could lead us to him." Max eyed the street. "We'll wait."

Max directed Jeremy to stand inside an office building about thirty feet from the coffee stand, while Bobby placed himself a few offices in the other direction. Max and Cassie waited in the car.

"You never answered my question." Max's deep voice penetrated the silence.

"What?" she said.

"I asked about you and Barnes."

She squared off at him. "I considered it a rhetorical question."

He continued to stare out the front window. "It wasn't."

"Not that it's any of your business, wait, what are we talking about here? I only met him two days ago. What do you think is going on between me and Jeremy?"

"I could guess."

He pressed his fist against his hip, the place where she suspected a piece of shrapnel had ripped the joint apart.

"Why?" she said.

"Excuse me?" His gaze seemed to look right through her, as though he didn't want to see her, or talk to her.

"Why do you care what I do or who I talk to?" she said.

"You smiled at him."

"Or who I smile at? It shouldn't matter a hoot. I should be able to smile at a bartender or a cop, or a male stripper for that matter."

He raised an eyebrow.

"Don't give me that look. I'm your assistant, not your little sister. You have no right to tell me who I can and cannot smile at. It's not in my job description."

"Stay here." Max whipped open the car door and casually strode to the espresso stand. What, did he need a sudden hit of caffeine to continue sparring with her?

Cassie wanted to give him a piece of her mind, but hesitated when she saw him nod at Jeremy. They were on the move.

Bobby Finn approached from the right, as Max faked a smile and spoke to the man in the sweatshirt. Jeremy started towards them. Max placed a friendly hand on the man's shoulder—

Sweatshirt guy spun around and swung at Max, who backed away. Max put his hand out, as if trying to reason with the man, calm him down. Cassie reached for the door handle, her heart racing into her throat. Sweatshirt guy lunged at Max, jabbing at him with his right hand. The afternoon sun reflected off something, momentarily blinding her.

God, no. Not a knife.

She clenched the door handle, frozen in place. He was going to stab Max, kill him right here in broad daylight on a busy Chicago street. Through her peripheral vision she saw pedestrians step back like a ripple around a stone plunking in water.

Sweatshirt guy yelled something, lunged again and

turned to run. Max tripped the guy with his cane and he fell flat to the sidewalk. Bobby jumped on top of him and pinned him to the cement. The knife? Where was the knife?

Her heartbeat hammered against her throat. Bobby grabbed sweatshirt guy by the shoulders and pressed him against the building. Bystanders slowed to get a better look. Jeremy approached, hands on his hips, speaking rationally, in complete control.

Max rolled his neck and joined Jeremy and Bobby as they questioned sweatshirt guy. She couldn't see him clearly, but realized he'd slid down the wall in surrender. Jeremy knelt down and talked with him, Bobby stood poised to subdue the man again, and Max leaned against the wall looking down, watching the interrogation.

She started to feel lightheaded and it was then she realized she'd been holding her breath. Glancing at her hand, she snapped it free of the door handle, berating herself for her trembling fingers. She'd healed, damn it, no longer that passive girl who let violence terrorize her.

Maybe it was still too soon. No, she wouldn't accept that. She'd grown a new set of emotional muscles to protect herself, an imaginary shield to keep the violence out.

Movement caught her eye. Two cops raced across the street and cuffed sweatshirt guy. One of the cops dragged him away, while the other stayed back and spoke with Jeremy. Bobby and Max headed for the car.

Breathe, Cassie. You don't want him to see you like this.

No, he'd send her packing for sure. But she couldn't leave, not yet. She had unfinished business in Chicago.

Bobby got behind the wheel. "That was bloody exciting. You okay, guv?"

Max slid onto the seat next to Cassie. "*Exciting* isn't the word that comes to mind."

He closed his eyes and tipped his head back.

"What happened, Bobby?" she asked.

"Bloody waste of time. He didn't know who paid him to drop off the note. He got the money at a phone box down the block. He walked by one day and the phone was ringing. He picked it up and was told to come back, same time tomorrow, and there'd be a note and a hundred-dollar bill waiting for him."

Jeremy got into the front seat and glanced at Cassie. "You okay back there?"

Max snapped his eyes open and studied her.

"Hey, don't worry about me," she said. "I'm fine. What about you? Didn't that guy have a knife or something?"

Max closed his eyes again. "Or something."

"Where to now?" Bobby asked.

"The command center," Max ordered.

"The hospital," Jeremy countered.

Max opened his eyes and glared at Jeremy.

"The hospital? Why?" Cassie panicked.

Then she looked at Max's fisted hand on the seat beside him. It was covered in blood.

Chapter Five

"A bloody waste of time," Max said, storming down the hospital corridor. "We've lost three hours on this case. I hope you're happy."

Jeremy wasn't happy. He was angry, frustrated and more than a bit worried about his senior in command. The man would have let himself bleed to death.

It wasn't as serious as Jeremy had suspected, but the team leader did need ten stitches. What was he planning to do, wrap it himself and risk infection?

Jeremy followed closely as his cranky ex-boss navigated around hospital personnel. It had been a boring three hours for sure, but necessary. Besides, there was no time clock going on this case…yet.

Max stopped short and turned to Jeremy. "I know what this is really about and I don't bloody like it. Deal with your own guilt. Don't use me to ease your conscience. I swear to God, if you keep treating me like a child I will hop the next plane to Seattle, C.K. be damned."

He rushed ahead, Bobby catching up to him. Jeremy counted to five before following, allowing Max space. Cassie kept pace with Jeremy.

"He doesn't mean it," she said.

"You're the expert, are you?" he smiled, half teasing. She shrugged.

He'd hoped letting her accompany Max into the examination room would help keep him calm. Jeremy guessed the last time Max had been in a hospital was for one of many surgeries to repair hip damage. A hospital was the last place Max would want ever to step foot into again. Jeremy couldn't blame him.

"It's not the pain. He doesn't do weakness very well," Cassie said.

"I'm sorry?"

"Y'know, the fact that he got stabbed is worse than the pain itself. He's probably ashamed he didn't defend himself better or some ridiculous thing like that."

Ridiculous? Like the guilt that settled low in Jeremy's gut? The guilt that screamed out: *If you'd been quicker you would have taken on the knife-wielding idiot instead of putting Max in his path.*

In two moves Jeremy could have disarmed him and avoided the bloodshed. Instead, the crippled former inspector had had to fend off the man.

If Max ever heard Jeremy refer to him as crippled, he'd strangle him with his bare hands.

Jeremy agreed with the girl, Max was berating

himself for letting the suspect get the better of him. Truth was, it could have happened to any of them. No one expected the man to go crazy and wave a switchblade wildly about. They didn't think him the killer, rather hoped he was a lead to the killer's identity.

"What guilt?" Cassie said.

Jeremy turned to her. "Excuse me?"

"Max said you needed to deal with your own guilt?"

His lips curled into a wry smile. Max had Jeremy's number on that one. "I was supposed to be at King's Cross Station when the bomb went off. Max was doing me a favor by picking up an agent. Max ended up in the hospital with a shattered hip, needing multiple operations. I ended up with his job."

"That's not your fault."

He didn't say anything. What could he say? That he'd spent the last ten months trying to work out how to make it up to Max, and now he feared he might be making the man's condition worse by thrusting him into the heat of another serial case?

"What is that all about?" Cassie said, slowing down.

Narrowing his eyes, Jeremy noticed a media crew on the other side of the glass doors.

"Looking for publicity, were you?" Max said to Jeremy.

"I had nothing to do with this."

"I'll get the car and bring it around." Bobby pushed through the group.

It was going to be tricky getting out of here without giving a statement.

"Why are they here?" Cassie said.

Max leaned against the wall, anger simmering beneath the surface. He didn't need this, didn't need one more distraction. The knife wound had been enough excitement for one afternoon.

"They must have heard about Blackwell," Barnes said.

Max eyed him. "Heard from whom?"

"Does it matter?"

"You sonofabitch."

"The car's here," Cassie said.

She put a hand to Max's arm for encouragement. He didn't move. He would not be photographed being dragged outside by this little slip of a thing.

"I can manage," he said.

He glared at Barnes. He wouldn't have called the press, would he? He wasn't that stupid. Or cruel.

The last time Max had had to deal with the press corps was the day of his resignation from Scotland Yard. The questions, the news cameras—the memory made him ill.

Just another hurdle, mate. Don't fall apart now.

Max pushed away from the wall and led them through the sliders and into the gang of vultures. He motioned for Cassie to get into the car.

Reporters fired questions at him:

"Mr. Templeton, can you tell us about the Blackwell Group?"

"Were you hired to find the man who murdered the two Jamison College students?"

"Do you think the man who stabbed you is the killer?"

Stand straight, shoulders erect, deep breaths. They can't hurt you, but they can hurt your case.

With Cassie safely in the back seat, he turned to the group. "Blackwell is a private organization. We're not bound by public information laws. In the best interest of our current investigation we won't be speaking with the press. Thank you."

The bright lights and incessant questions paralyzed him for a second. He was back in London, unable to answer the critical question: *Why haven't you made an arrest?*

Something tugged on his jacket. He glanced down, into the sweet, round face of his assistant.

"Get in the car," she said.

As if in a dream he did as ordered, then closed the door. Lights flashed through the windows and the chaos continued, even as Bobby sped away from the curb.

"Unfortunate," Barnes said.

"Then why did you phone them?" Max accused.

His second in command turned to look at Max. "Why would I phone them, Max? I have nothing to gain by their involvement."

"How about self-promotion?"

"If that's what you think." Barnes turned his back to him.

No, Max didn't think Jeremy would sabotage the case by involving the local press. It was old resentment and frustration that took him down that road. Max sensed that Jeremy had changed since their days at SCI. He seemed less arrogant, humbled even.

Guilt did that to a person.

If that were the case, Max would be a saint by now.

"Hey, guv, maybe the Patron released a media statement to open some doors for us." Bobby glanced into the rearview.

"More likely one of the Chicago cops let it slip," Jeremy said.

"Why?" Cassie asked.

"Territorial issues."

She looked at Jeremy, waiting for more of an explanation. Max jumped in. "The locals aren't thrilled by Blackwell's presence here. It makes them look incompetent."

Which is exactly how Max felt after being bested by that punk. The kid couldn't have been a day over twenty, a pawn used to play a killer's game with Max and the team. How did he let that twit get the best of him? It was obvious the kid didn't know how to use the weapon he'd brandished. He'd admitted as much when he'd confessed to borrowing it from a cousin for protection against loan sharks. The kid's biggest crime was betting money he didn't have.

That, and following a directive from a stranger on the other end of a telephone line.

He fisted his left hand, the blood pumping to his wound, setting it on fire. He should have taken a Vicodin, as ordered, but he hated being dependent on drugs. He couldn't even bring himself to take the sleep medications prescribed to stop the nightmares.

No, Max was a sucker for self-torture.

"Why did he stab you?" Cassie said.

Max glanced at her. "It was an accident."

"He was accidentally carrying a butcher knife?"

"It wasn't a butcher knife." He studied her, suddenly realizing what a sod he'd been. She was most likely terrorized by the incident and all he could think about was his bruised ego. "He borrowed it to protect himself from loan sharks."

"Which he assumed you were because…?"

"Who knows." Max glanced out the window. It was rush hour and traffic had slowed.

"It's the beard," she said.

"Can't you get off that crusade?"

"I'm trying to help."

"The knifer did say you reminded him of his paroled cousin," Jeremy added.

"You're all out to get me," Max joked, going along with the lighter mood.

They were all frustrated by the dead end. It did no good to wallow in disappointment. In his days as team leader at SCI, Max worked diligently to keep the boys motivated. With the proper attitude they could solve most any crime.

"Bobby," Max said. "What do you think? Should I trim the whiskers?"

"Ah, I dunno, guv, is it a turn-on for the ladies?"

Max turned to Cassie. "Well, do I hurt my chances with the ladies or improve them if I shave this off?" He ran his fingers across his beard.

"Shave it off." She winked.

If he didn't know better he'd think she was flirting with him. It couldn't be. She was a sweet girl with a horrific past. The last man she'd be interested in was a man like Max: heavy on angst, light on humor.

"That's it then," he said. "Maybe a shave will turn this whole case around."

CASSIE WOKE UP to complete blackness. The glow of a streetlight peered through a crack in the curtains stretched across her window. What time was it? Where was she again? Right, Chicago.

And she was okay, safe.

Sitting up, she stretched her arms over her head and glanced at the clock. Eight o'clock. She'd meant to take a quick nap, maybe twenty minutes. Instead, she'd been asleep for two hours.

She must have needed the rest from her full afternoon: witnessing the knifing and trying to keep Max from climbing the walls at the hospital. Emotionally spent, she'd welcomed the down time to recharge her batteries.

Her stomach growled. She'd slept right through

dinner, and had barely eaten her lunch, thanks to the emergency call about the note.

"Face it, girl, you're all outta whack."

Being around Max, trying to keep him grounded, had drained her somehow.

Not good. She felt old habits rising, self-sacrificing, caretaking habits that completely blinded her to the realities of life. She found herself wanting to heal Max, even if that meant putting herself at risk. No, she'd come too far to fall back into that kind of doormat behavior.

She'd have to watch herself.

She went down the hall to the bathroom, brushed her hair and washed her face. Hoping someone had stocked the refrigerator with food, she started down the stairs. Yeah, who was she kidding? She was living in a houseful of men. Their idea of food was ordering a pizza.

With a sigh, she passed the main area of the command center and spotted Eddie hunched over his computer, asleep.

She took a step into the room and caught herself. She had to stop being responsible for the entire world, or at least her portion of it.

"I tried to get him to go home, but he'd have none of it."

She turned at the sound of Max's soft voice. Her breath caught in her throat. He'd shaved all right. His bare skin defined his high cheekbones and full, perfectly shaped lips. She noticed a scar along his left jawline and she wondered if it was from the bombing.

"Well, say something." He half smiled.

He almost sounded nervous.

"Wow," she said.

"That's it?"

"I mean, you look different." She couldn't help the admiration in her voice.

"You'd no longer peg me as a loan shark?"

"No, definitely no, I mean, not."

"Good. You hungry?" he said.

"Yeah."

"I've got leftovers in the kitchen."

She followed him down the hallway, marveling at the new, improved version of her boss. Not only did he look like a million bucks, but he also acted almost human…like a gentleman.

"Where is everybody?" she said.

"I sent Barnes, Finn and McDonald to a pub to relax for a few hours. Relieving the pressure makes us more productive in the long run. Kreegan went home to be with her family. Spinelli's following up on a lead."

He pulled out a foil package from the refrigerator. "Pizza okay? I guess it's the specialty around here."

She peeked inside the foil. "Deep-dish. My favorite."

It had been years since she'd had decent pizza. Karl had told her it would make her fat and soft. Deep-dish pizza was one more thing she'd given up along with her self-esteem when she'd married the SOB. If she'd only known.

But how could she? At eighteen, she'd been ripe for someone older and wiser to take care of her and help her escape the hell of her own house. Karl had been perfect at first: seven years older, with a stable job and worldly experience. She'd admired him, thought she'd loved him.

Yeah, like a prisoner loved its captor.

"What, you don't like sausage?" he said.

She glanced into Max's green eyes. He'd been watching her.

"Love sausage, thanks. I'll get the plate."

"No, no. Sit down."

She hesitated. A man waiting on her?

Leaning on his cane, he moved to the counter and pulled a plate from the cabinet. It couldn't be easy holding the plate while balancing on his cane. She started to go to him.

She stopped herself. She could tell he wanted to do this for her.

He put the pizza on a plate and popped it in the microwave.

"How about an ale?" He clenched his jaw as he went to the refrigerator.

"Sure, light beer?"

"Ah, Americans. What you need is a pint of Guinness after a day like this."

He twisted off the top and placed a bottle of light beer in front of her. "Glass?" He turned.

"No, I like it out of the bottle."

Actually, she rarely drank beer, but didn't want to offend him. He was trying so hard.

"Pizza's got a few minutes." He sat next to her at the kitchen table. "Do you have any regrets?"

"About what?"

"Coming to Chicago with me?"

"No," Cassie said.

"I don't believe you."

He'd meant it teasingly, but she heard Karl's voice: *I don't believe you, you bitch. Who were you screwing around with when I was in Detroit?*

She fingered her gold heart locket, the only keepsake she'd taken with her when she'd left her family.

"What is that charm around your neck?" he asked.

She didn't want to tell him at first. Too intimate.

"Just a locket my mom gave me," she said.

"It seems like more than *just* a locket," Max said, shooting her a half smile.

He looked downright dangerous tonight, sexy as hell with a hint of vulnerability. She found herself wanting to run from the room.

"It's got fairy dust inside," she said. "When I was a kid, Mom told me if I was ever in trouble to open the locket and the fairy dust would help me fly away."

"That's lovely," he said.

Cassie had believed the story up until the night Karl had sent her tumbling down a flight of stairs. She could have used wings that night.

"Is it too painful, coming back to Chicago?" he asked.

"No, I don't regret coming back," she said, not looking at him. She didn't want him to read pain in her eyes. He'd blame himself, and the man didn't need any more complications, like feeling responsible for Cassie's angst. "It's a little harder than I thought it would be."

"The memories?"

"Yep." She glanced up at him.

He leaned back in the chair and crossed his arms over his chest. "I've heard the best way to deal with bad memories is to confront them head-on. Prove to yourself that they can't hurt you anymore."

"And you've tried this technique yourself, inspector?" she joked.

"No, not yet." Regret colored his voice. "Someday."

A few seconds of silence passed.

"I would like to see my mom while I'm here." She leaned against the table. "It's been over a year."

He leaned forward and placed his hand to her shoulder. Her breath caught. He seemed so different, so kind and gentle.

Without thinking, she reached up and touched his scar. He didn't move away or scold her. He looked almost fragile, as if he might break into pieces.

"What's this from?" she said, barely able to get the

words out. Her fingers warmed as though she cradled a cup of hot cocoa. But it was only his skin, rough yet soft, the scar a slight discoloration against his stubbled jaw.

The microwave beeped.

"Your pizza," he said.

"Okay," she answered.

Neither moved.

She thought he was going to kiss her.

She wanted him to kiss her.

The front door burst open and the echo of male voices broke their spell. She shot up from her chair and went to get her pizza.

What just happened? She leaned into the counter and took a deep breath, then pulled her pizza from the microwave.

"I swear she was hitting on me," Bobby boasted from the hallway.

"You wish," Art McDonald countered. "Hey, guv," he said, coming into the kitchen.

"It's Sleeping Beauty," Bobby said.

Cassie turned to greet them. "Hi," she said, still recovering from her moment with Max.

"Good morning, love. You okay?" Bobby walked over to her. "You're lookin' a little pale. You been tangling with our esteemed leader again?"

"No, I'm fine."

"Maybe you're catching something." Bobby placed the back of his hand to her forehead.

It was a pleasant enough touch, but not warm and hypnotic like Max's.

"I was worn out from all the excitement." Plate in hand, she went to the table and sat by Max.

"You don't know the half of it, love." Bobby started toward her, but Max shot him a look that stopped the man in mid-stride. "We're all famous, we are," Bobby added.

"Which is why he thinks women were hitting on him at McGreevy's Pub," Art added.

"Famous?" She nibbled on her pizza.

"We were on the telly. Showed us coming out of the hospital. You looked great, guv," Bobby said. "They only showed me through the car window. Wish they'd caught my good side." Bobby turned his cheek.

"You don't have a good side," Art said.

"I do too, you bloody ox. Leave me alone, I'm famous."

"If you're famous then I'm the prime minister."

"You'd do a better job of it," Bobby shot back.

"Enough," Max said. "Barnes, you're awfully quiet. What, no ladies hit on you tonight?"

She glanced at Jeremy. He leaned against the wall, his arms crossed over his chest. He looked…troubled, and definitely sober.

"It wasn't for lack of trying," Bobby answered for him. "He had at least four beauties try to buy him a pint, but he was having none of it. He sulked in the corner sipping his tonic, that one."

"And draws them like flies, yeah?" Max said.

Jeremy's expression didn't change and he didn't open his mouth to participate in the conversation. He was such a controlled, detached man. That control could eat him up from the inside.

"I need a pint." Bobby opened the fridge. "What's this? No Guinness?"

"I got them home safe, guv," Jeremy said. "I'm heading up to read."

Bobby closed the refrigerator door. "You're going to read?"

"Good night," Jeremy said and started down the hall.

"Reading is so bloody boring," Bobby called after him. "You're never going to catch a girl by reading and drinking tonic."

"Come on, Bobby," Art said, an arm around his partner. "Let's see if there's anything good on the telly. They've got BBC America. Maybe we'll get lucky and catch a Benny Hill repeat."

"But—" he protested.

"Come on, let's leave these two in peace." Art smiled at Cassie. "Good night, miss, guv."

"Thanks, Art," Max said.

She nibbled at her pizza, listening to Bobby argue about women with Art. Art, she guessed ten years Bobby's senior, was married with teenage children. Bobby, late twenties, was a committed bachelor, and maybe even a ladies' man. Or at least he thought himself one.

"Sorry about that," Max said.

She glanced up and found him studying her intently. "Actually, all the commotion is kind of nice."

"You live alone?"

"Yeah."

"Me, too," he said.

He rolled his eyes, as if he'd uttered the stupidest thing ever because, of course, she knew he lived alone. She knew most everything about him. To ease the tension, she changed the subject.

"I didn't think I'd miss it so much," she said.

"What?"

"Chicago. Well, not the city, exactly, but I miss the snow, I miss the pizza," she chuckled, motioning to her plate. "I miss…" She stopped short.

How could she describe it? She couldn't miss something she'd never had. Her childhood had been fraught with tension and violence, Dad hitting Mom for not making dessert or not ironing his shirts properly, Mom hiding the girls when he had his drunken rages. She'd taken the brunt of the brutality.

Only years later, after Cassie had experienced the abuse firsthand from Karl, did she understand how a woman would let herself become victimized.

"What do you miss?" Max pushed.

"I miss my mom." Cassie'd never got to say thanks for keeping her and her sisters out of harm's way. "I should go see her."

"I could come with you, if you'd like."

He meant well, but the offer bothered her. Not just bothered her, threatened her. She didn't want him getting too close, knowing too much about her life. She didn't want his support. Besides, bringing a man home with her would indicate a seriousness in their relationship that didn't exist. A seriousness that could never exist.

He was a wounded man in a violent career, two major red flags for a girl like Cassie.

"Thanks," she said. "But I have to do this alone."

Chapter Six

Two hours later, Max found himself headed to the fire escape for a smoke. He and Cassie had said their good-nights an hour ago, acknowledging that they had an early morning and long day ahead of them. Next up: a visit to the fraternity.

He passed Barnes's room. A shaft of light streamed through the two-inch crack and classical music drifted into the hallway. Max had half a mind to scold him about disturbing his neighbors. He pushed open the door. Barnes was asleep in the corner chair, a book open in his lap, his specs lying on top. Max closed the door.

He passed the TV room where Bobby slept soundly on the couch. Art reclined in the lounger watching a repeat of *Monty Python*. The man had changed into a powder-blue track suit with a double white stripe running down the sides.

"Hey, guv," Art whispered, not wanting to wake Bobby. "Can't sleep?"

"Needed a bedtime smoke."

Art nodded. "Did you see the media clip from this afternoon?"

"I saw it." He wasn't happy about it. They didn't need the spotlight—it would only complicate the investigation.

"Your girl looked pretty on the telly. I meant to tell her she should go out for advertisements."

"I hadn't noticed."

Liar.

"Well, you go on and enjoy your smoke. God, I wish I could sleep. It's the bloody jet lag."

"Doesn't seem to bother Bobby." Max smiled.

"Neither did the three pints he had at the pub. Maybe I should start drinking."

Max narrowed his eyes.

"Just kidding," Art said. "I'm too old."

"Night, then."

"Good night, guv."

Max continued toward the fire escape. He'd have to pass Cassie's room, which was down the hallway by the fire escape door. She was probably fast asleep. Good. He didn't want to struggle with small talk, as he had earlier.

What is the matter with you?

For some reason, sitting in the kitchen and watching her eat pizza had felt incredibly odd, almost intimate. He'd never eaten with her like that before, the two of them sitting at a kitchen table, inches apart. Sure, she'd be working at his flat during lunchtime, but she'd always brought a sandwich to eat at her desk. She'd never asked for a break.

Suddenly he felt like an absolute wanker.

He wanted to apologize, but how? Admit he'd been a complete idiot during their four-month relationship? No, he wouldn't call it a relationship, more like a business partnership. He'd paid her money and she'd typed out his story. But she'd also done more than that: she ran errands, made meals on occasion, and even picked up the flat. She didn't have to do that.

And he hadn't stopped her. No, somewhere, deep down, he appreciated the human gestures, welcomed them. He'd done such a good job of isolating himself that he'd forgotten what it felt like to have someone care about him.

Think again, Templeton. She's being paid for her trouble, remember?

Still, he felt an apology was in order. He approached her room and noticed light reflecting from under the door.

"What, doesn't anyone sleep anymore?" He knocked softly. "Cassie, may I come in?"

He waited. Nothing.

"Cassie?" He tried again.

The hair bristled on the back of his neck. She was a high-energy sort, the kind who would jump from her chair if she heard something. Maybe from years of being ready to defend herself from an abuser?

He tried the knob. The door was open. If she'd

fallen asleep while reading, Max could be a sport and turn the light off.

"Cassie," he whispered, pushing open the door. He took a step inside and froze. The perfectly made bed was empty.

"What the hell?" he said. Did she go back downstairs for some warm milk? He glanced out the fire escape window to see if the light from the kitchen reflected out back. It didn't.

He stepped into her room looking for clues as to her whereabouts. A picture frame had been turned down on her nightstand. He set it back up and studied the photograph: a mother and three little girls.

Cassie had said she wanted to see her mum, but he didn't think she'd meant tonight. *Forget it, mate.* She'd made her feelings clear on that one: she didn't want Max anywhere near her family.

He couldn't blame her. What a shock for her mum, not to see her daughter for over a year, then receiving a surprise visit complete with Max, a mess of a bloke with a limp and odd mental illness. Wouldn't fill Mum with confidence that her daughter had healed and was making better choices about men.

He phoned her mobile from the house line. Voice mail picked up.

"Bloody hell." He scanned her room, analyzing its contents: a blue and white blanket that looked too worn not to be hers, and a teddy bear on the bed. He picked it up. Guilt grabbed hold of his conscience. He shouldn't be here touching her private things.

Putting it back to the bed, he glanced across the room at a journal lying open on top of the telly.

...she looked pretty on the telly...should go out for advertisements...meant to tell her...

Panic flooded his chest. Blast, another attack. He leaned against the wall and willed himself not to fall apart in the girl's room. He wouldn't let her find him like this, sweating, trembling, collapsed in a heap. He backed out of the room and closed the door, his hand gripping the glass handle with deadly force as he tried to ground himself.

Her earlier words echoed in his brain: *My ex-husband broke my back, put me in the hospital for two months and tracked me down at my sister's when I got out.*

What if that bastard saw her on the telly tonight? Recognized her, decided a reunion was in order while she was in town?

Max went downstairs in search of Eddie. The computer genius's desk was empty. Max pounded his fist against the doorjamb.

Then he heard snoring from the other room. He went to the back den and found Eddie sound asleep on the leather couch.

"Eddie, wake up," Max ordered.

"I'm not late!" Eddie bolted straight up, his eyes wide.

"Easy, mate, I need your help."

Eddie stared into Max's eyes. Was the man even fully awake?

"Help? Help?" Eddie mimicked.

"I need you to help me find Cassie."

"Cassie, right," He rubbed his eyes. "Cute, blond, nice ass."

Max refrained from boxing his ears. "If she needed a cab, which one would she ring?"

"Yellow. Mellow yellow."

"Come on, wake up." He shook the kid's shoulder.

"I'm awake! I'm awake! Yellow Cab. Everyone calls Yellow Cab."

Max stood. "Phone books, do we have phone books?"

"I dunno." He rubbed his eyes. "I get all my numbers online."

"Get it then, Yellow Cab."

"Okay, okay." He got up and headed to his desk. "Never pegged you for a late-night drinker."

"What's that?"

"You're meeting Cassie at a bar, right? Don't waste your money on a cab. Take my car."

"Sit," Max ordered. "Now find me that number for Yellow Cab."

Eddie settled behind his desk. "It's gonna take me a minute."

Max glared.

"Hey, Tabitha was asleep. She needs a minute to get her bearings."

"Tabitha?"

Eddie motioned toward his laptop. "Tabitha, meet my boss, Max Templeton." Eddie smiled.

And they thought Max was crazy.

"The number," Max ordered.

Eddie punched a few keys, hit Return and a Web site came up. "Damn."

"What?"

"Web site's down. Hang on." His fingers flew over the keyboard, and he leaned back in his chair. "Come on, sweetheart, the boss needs to find a woman."

Panic still burned in Max's gut. Cassie could be in trouble.

Or Max was overreacting and had completely gone round the bend.

"Here," Eddie leaned forward. "You've got four numbers, take your pick."

Max grabbed Eddie's desk phone and punched in a number. He got a recording. "Bloody hell."

"When you find her, take my car," Eddie offered again.

"What, and drive on the wrong side of the road? No thanks." He'd never mastered the skill of driving in the States, and surely didn't want to navigate Chicago motorways.

Max tried another number.

"Yellow Cab."

"Yes, my wife just left and I need to know where her

cab was going. Did you have a pickup at 102 Cedar within the last hour?"

"I can't tell you that. Do you want a cab or not?"

"It's an emergency."

"It's against company policy."

"But—"

"I'm sorry, sir."

CLICK.

"Your wife?" Eddie eyed Max.

Okay, he couldn't do this alone. "Cassie's gone and I've got to find her, immediately."

"O-kay." Eddie raised a brow.

"It's not like that. I'm worried about her," Max said. He didn't know where the words came from, and couldn't believe he'd uttered them to a complete stranger.

He should have ordered the kid to find her, threatened his job if he didn't.

"What's her last name?" Eddie said, readjusting his fingers to the keyboard.

"Clarke, but it may not be her real name."

Eddie glanced up at him.

"She's got a rather complicated past."

"Don't we all," Eddie muttered. "Okay, the cab company, let's assume it was Yellow Cab. Wait, what about her cell phone?"

"She isn't answering." Max paced to the front window.

He wasn't sure why, but he needed to get to her. Or was this another anxiety attack from the post-trauma affliction?

"Got it!" Eddie said. "Found the pickup—ten thirty, destination…Des Plaines."

"Where's that?"

"Northwest suburb."

"Order me a cab. I need to change."

Max went upstairs and dressed in crisp trousers and a white shirt, in case he did meet the family. He glanced in the bedroom mirror to determine if he looked presentable.

"Hopeless," he muttered.

He went downstairs and grabbed his leather jacket from a chair. Eddie came up beside him.

"The cab's outside, yeah?" Max said.

"Nope. I'm driving." Eddie put up his hand in defense. "No arguments, boss. That's what friends do for each other. My truck's in the alley."

Eddie shoved a baseball cap onto his unruly head of black hair and made for the back of the house. Max followed.

Friends? What a strange concept. Max had lost anything resembling friendship after the bombing, mostly by choice. He didn't want them feeling obliged to help him, check on him…feel sorry for him.

They got into Late Eddie's car, a compact SUV, and pulled out of the alley. Max tapped a fisted hand against his knee. He was overreacting, that's all. Fine, if that be the case, he'd get to Cassie's mum's house, watch from outside, maybe offer her a ride home and all would be well.

"Music, okay?" Eddie said.

"Sure."

The kid hit a button and the rubbish they called country music blared through the car. Although it was popular in England, Max had never warmed to it.

"Sorry," Eddie said, turning it down.

"You know where you're going?" Max asked.

"Ran directions off the Net."

They drove in relative silence except for the sound of the music. Friends were too much work, Max thought, gritting his teeth. He couldn't bring himself to ask Eddie to switch to another station. The guy was doing him a grand favor by taking him on this midnight adventure.

"I always wanted to be a cowboy," Eddie said, his head bobbing with the music.

Max glanced at him. Was this supposed to be true confessions, then?

"What happened?" Max said, to be polite.

"Allergic to hay."

Max nodded, then glanced out the passenger window. Lyrics from the radio filled the car…lyrics about love, hope and dreams.

Now he knew why he'd never warmed to country music.

"What did you want to be?" Eddie asked.

Max wanted to tell him it was none of his business, to focus on the road and get him to Cassie before something dreadful happened. *You're overreacting, mate.*

"I always wanted to be a detective," Max said.

"Luck-y," Eddie muttered.

Is that what you'd call Max's life? Lucky? He wouldn't go there with this kid, a young man who exuded an innocence that Max envied.

Innocence.

Innocent children, mothers being strewn about the train station like paper dolls.

Shove it back, mate.

He closed his eyes…

…and saw Cassie's sweet, round face smiling at him.

She, too, wore an innocence, even after everything she'd been through. How did she do it? How did she keep a positive outlook on life after the abuse she'd survived?

She puzzled him, that one. She seemed to be fragile beauty and independent strength all in one. But then, he probably puzzled her, too.

Or maybe not, maybe she had him sussed out, knew he hid from his life by snapping and growling and acting like a supreme ass.

It was best this way. It kept him a safe distance from people.

"I grew up a few towns over from Des Plaines." Eddie glanced at Max, then back to the road. "How about you?"

"I'm not much for small talk, mate," Max said.

Eddie shrugged. Was that chagrin creasing the boy's brow?

"Coventry." Max looked at him. "England."

"I figured as much." He chuckled. "What brought you over here?"

A sardonic smile creased Max's lips. "A woman."

"Nice," Eddie said in appreciation.

"It didn't work out. Take my advice, never let a woman dictate your life."

"First I gotta get a woman."

Max studied his driver. The boy seemed nice enough, youthful in some ways, above-average looks, although that hairstyle could scare anyone away. He had a full head of curls that made him look wild and immature.

"So, why are we tailing Cassie?" Eddie asked.

Max's smile faded and he stared straight ahead. "Let's just get there."

"Sure, okay, boss."

The reference to Cassie brought him back down, sinking him in a mass of panic.

She'll be okay. Yet the panic in his chest proved otherwise.

The trouble was he was going mad.

Thirty minutes later they pulled onto a residential street lined with small brick houses. Eddie parked across the street from the house where the cab supposedly dropped off Cassie. The house was completely dark.

Max reread the address. They were at the right house. "You're sure this is where the cab brought her?"

"I'm sure," Eddie said, eyeing the small home.

"She wouldn't have left already."

"Whose house is it, anyway?" Eddie asked.

"Her mother's. Hasn't seen her in over a year."

"Intense."

Max got out of the car and eyed the neighboring homes.

"Hey, boss, over there in the park."

Max glanced across the street where he noticed a man and a woman. The man gripped the woman by the wrist.

"Let go!" the woman demanded.

Max's blood ran cold.

"Cassie," he whispered.

Chapter Seven

"I missed you so much, honey," Karl crooned. "I figured you'd come home."

The jerk had seen Cassie in the Blackwell news report and he'd been waiting for her at Mom's house, Mom's old house. She no longer lived there. Sadness crept into Cassie's chest.

"I never should have let you go," he said. "I've missed you. I never meant to hurt you."

Like he was hurting her now? Squeezing her wrist like he wanted juice from an orange?

"I've missed you so much," he whispered and pulled her against him.

"Don't touch me!" she cried, kicking him in the shin to break the hold.

In slow motion she saw it coming, his unwieldy, large hand aiming for her cheek.

Instead of cowering, as she would have in the past, she grabbed his wrist, twisted and jerked him off balance. She kicked in the back of his knee, he fell to the ground and she kicked him in the ribs.

"You're friggin' nuts," he cried, rolling away from her.

She kept after him, kicking him in the chest, adrenaline blinding her. Then someone grabbed her by the waist and pulled her away from Karl.

"Cassie?" It was Max's voice.

Shame curdled in her belly. Max placed a hand to her cheek and looked into her eyes.

"It's okay." Max brushed his thumb across her cheek, his concerned expression touching her somewhere, deep down where the violence hadn't reached. "Take her to the car," he ordered his companion. She glanced over her shoulder into the compassionate eyes of Eddie.

Great. More people knew her shame: she'd fallen for a bastard who had broken her...and she'd let him.

Max nodded and Eddie led her to an SUV. She climbed into the back seat. "He hurt me," she choked.

"It's okay now." Eddie squeezed her shoulder and closed the door.

She clasped her hands together, her fingers shaking as if she'd been exposed to the cold for hours, days even. A tear slipped down her cheek and she felt her lower lip quiver. That crazed animal that attacked Karl wasn't her. She was a nurturer, a sweet girl.

Well, she had been a sweet girl for a brief time, when her first months with Karl had been blissful and perfect.

Now it was back to being guarded and cynical, the way she was growing up.

There'd been another brief time, during the past year, when she'd caught glimpses of a sweeter, happier self, glimpses of a girl with hope in her heart.

Tonight that girl was completely lost and Max had showed up in time to witness her rage. She didn't want him to see her that way, out of control and violent.

Why had he come, anyway?

He opened the door and got into the back seat beside her. "He won't be bothering you anymore."

"I didn't need your help," she said.

"Obviously. All the same, are you hurt?"

He reached over and examined her wrist, where there would surely be bruises tomorrow. Such a tender, caring touch in contrast to Karl's. But she didn't welcome Max's touch or attention. She didn't want to depend on any man. For anything.

She snapped her wrist back. "Don't."

The look on his face tore at her heart.

"Let's get back, Eddie," Max ordered.

"You got it, boss."

They pulled away from the curb and Max closed himself off to her, staring out his window. She hadn't meant to snap at him, but her emotions were splattered across her chest thanks to the encounter with Karl. Truth was, she'd never thought she'd see him again.

After the "accident" that had put her in the hospital,

she'd pressed charges, filed papers and kept the nurse-call button close at hand while recovering. She thought Karl had gotten the message, but months later he'd showed up at her sister's house, begging for forgiveness and claiming to have enrolled in an anger management program.

When her father suggested she give Karl another chance, she truly saw what had happened. She'd learned how to love from her mother, how to love an abuser, and if she went back to Karl, she'd end up like her mother: fearful, lost and bruised in more places than she'd ever admit.

Cassie always wondered why Mom stayed with the old man, but deep down she had her suspicions. Mom didn't have a college degree or training of any kind. She was a good housewife and a loving mother. She needed her husband's paycheck to provide for her girls.

She'd sacrificed her life for them.

And Cassie wanted to thank her, yet she hadn't a clue where Mom had gone.

Had she divorced Dad? Where were Cassie's sisters? Did Lindsy make it into University of Illinois as planned? Did Bethany and Mark move to Florida for his job?

Cassie didn't know. She didn't know because she'd thought keeping in touch with them would put them in danger from her ex-husband.

Sure, he'd been remorseful when he'd tried convincing her of his love over a year ago. He'd practically broken down, swearing never to hurt her again.

She'd heard those words before. God, she'd been so stupid.

It always started the same way. A suggestion, turned into an order, followed by punishment if the order was not obeyed. She should have recognized trouble when he'd wanted the names and addresses of her girlfriends, then when he started showing up at the girls' night out with his buddies. At first she'd thought it cute. But as time passed, it started to bother her.

Just like it bothered her when he talked about having children. At first she'd said her female "issues" were too volatile to consider pregnancy. Fibroids were painful and could be complicated. But as the years passed, she knew it was something else that kept her on birth control pills, something that motivated her to hide them for fear that if Karl found her taking birth control he'd flip out.

Listen to yourself, girl. Why did you stay with him so long?

Because it's what she knew. Because she thought *that* was love.

Thank God she knew better now. She knew what love *wasn't*. Yet she wouldn't recognize true love if it was gift-wrapped and dropped in her lap.

"Great news about the note, hey, boss?"

Eddie's voice splintered her thoughts.

"What news?" she said.

"The specks on the note weren't blood," Max said, not looking at her.

She owed him an apology, an explanation for pushing him away. No she didn't. She'd told him that she needed to see her mother alone.

"Why did you come?" she pushed. She resented the fact that she'd been relieved to see him.

Max clenched his jaw and stared out the window.

"How did you find me?" she said.

"I found you," Eddie offered, smiling into the rearview mirror. "The boss woke me from a sound sleep and said he was worried about you, so we called the Yellow Cab company, but they wouldn't give up the information, so I did my magic and broke into their system and—"

"Why?" she interrupted his ramble and studied Max. "Why were you worried about me?"

"It doesn't matter."

"You didn't think I could take care of myself, did you?"

They pulled into the alley behind the house and Eddie parked. Max got out and slammed the door.

She jumped out after him. "Wait a second."

He was halfway up the back stairs when she caught up to him. "We're not done," she said.

"I think we are. You've made your feelings clear, Miss Clarke."

Eddie stood at the bottom of the steps looking from Cassie to Max.

"Inside," Max ordered Eddie, not taking his eyes off Cassie.

"Sure thing, boss." Eddie glanced at Cassie. "Glad

you're okay. Good night." He disappeared into the house. Max stood opposite her, leaning into his cane.

"How's your hip?" she said.

He shook his head and started up the steps.

"Max, wait."

He didn't turn, didn't look at her. Shame gripped her vocal cords. She had to do this.

"I'm kind of messed up right now," she said. "I didn't expect to see him."

"And now you have. You've conquered your demons all by yourself. Congratulations."

"Max," she croaked.

He turned slowly and looked at her. Tears welled up in her eyes, tears of frustration and loss. She wanted to tell him she'd lost her family, possibly for good, and the pain was unbearable.

No words came out.

She started up the stairs and he touched her shoulder. "What is it?" he said.

She leaned into his chest, her fingers clutching his cotton shirt like a child squeezing a stuffed animal. His deep, earthy scent filled her head, welcoming her, making her feel safe and grounded.

Weak, you're a weak and foolish broad. Karl's voice rang in her head.

She broke the embrace. "I told you I'm a mess." Her chuckle came out more like a cough. She rushed to the back door.

"Cassie?"

She hesitated, studying the chipped window frame trimming the glass.

"Look at me," Max said.

She was afraid to, afraid of what she'd see in his eyes.

"Please?" he said.

She turned, biting her lower lip. But she didn't read disappointment or disgust on his face. She read compassion, and that scared her even more.

"Can I help?" he said.

She shook her head no, swallowed back a ball of emotion and went into the house. She'd spent the last year and a half learning to depend on no one but herself. Yet she'd welcomed his touch of support, falling into his arms and leaning against his strong, hard chest.

He was the first person she'd felt slightly inclined to lean on.

She couldn't allow that. She sensed Max was a man she could grow dependent on.

"No," she whispered. She'd made herself a promise never to fall into that trap again. Besides, he had enough baggage of his own. He didn't need hers.

She raced up the stairs to her bedroom, needing to get away from him, to forget what happened and find peace. How was she going to do that when his caring, green eyes and soft, deep voice would surely haunt her dreams?

THE NEXT MORNING, Max walked into the kitchen and aimed for the coffee. He needed the caffeine to make up for a total of four hours of sleep. He poured some into a large Chicago Bears mug and settled himself at the kitchen table. Someone had had the presence of mind to bring in the morning paper. He flipped a few pages and his eyes caught on a headline: Private Task Force Hunts Serial Killer.

"Bloody Nora!" He slammed his fist to the table.

Footsteps echoed down the hall. Barnes stepped into the kitchen and aimed for the kettle. "You're awfully loud first thing in the morning."

"We're in the paper. Did you see it?"

"I saw it," Barnes said, in a monotone voice.

Barnes rarely showed emotion. Max envied the man's self-control.

"We don't need the publicity," Max said. "It's only going to muddle the investigation."

Barnes didn't respond.

"Is everybody here?" Max wanted to get started, frustrated that they'd wasted a full day chasing their tails.

"It's just seven. I expect they'll be down soon." He turned to Max. "I tried to rouse Late Eddie from his spot in the den, but he's out cold."

"He had a late night," Max said.

Barnes raised a brow.

"He and I went out."

"Really? Trolling the pubs for women?"

"Not exactly. We were looking for Cassie," Max explained.

"What, she went missing?"

"She went to visit family and I got worried."

"Why?"

"It's a long story," Max said. "Wake everyone, will you?"

"But I—" He glanced at the teakettle, then back to Max. "Right."

He strode past Max.

"Wait. Barnes?"

Barnes hesitated at the door and looked through his rimless specs at him.

"Don't wake Cassie," Max said. "She can join us when she's ready."

"Yes, sir."

He disappeared into the hallway and Max heard him climb the stairs to the second floor.

She went to visit family and I got worried.

Why?

That one word haunted Max. Cassie had asked him the same question: Why was he worried about her last night?

Because after nearly a year of shutting himself off from the world, he'd finally started to care about someone: his little blond assistant.

A lot of good it did him. When he'd found Cassie it was obvious Max was the last person she wanted around, and it was even more obvious she didn't need his help.

He'd been stunned when she'd lost it and attacked her ex-husband with such voracity. She would have kept on hitting and kicking him. It was a good thing Max showed up when he did. At least it kept her from being arrested. Max made sure of that. While Late Eddie took her to the car, Max had a proper chat with her ex, explaining the ramifications if he filed a police report.

Max said he had influence with the local police and they wouldn't believe a word of his complaint. He also said that Cassie had moved on, to which the man said, "With a cripple?" Max had smiled and hadn't disagreed. He let the bastard think she'd found an even bigger bastard to fall in love with.

Max finished by explaining that Cassie was part of a team of professionals that included former detectives from Scotland Yard and the Chicago Police. The ex would have to get past all of them to talk to her again. Max suggested he move on with his life; Cassie wanted no part of it.

When Max started toward the car, he'd heard the ex come up behind him. Max stepped aside and stuck out his cane, effectively sending the twit facedown on the sidewalk. With the tip of his cane to the back of the man's neck, Max leveled one last warning, then headed for the car. The ex didn't follow, most likely ashamed at being bested by a "cripple."

Max pushed back from the kitchen table and limped to the coffeepot. Late Eddie could use a strong cup of coffee with the night he'd had. He'd really come through for Max.

Max poured a mug of coffee, his gaze drifting to the spot outside where Cassie had leaned into his chest last night. He wasn't sure how to comfort her, so he'd stood there, feeling her heart beat against his chest, his own heart breaking a little as she rubbed her cheek against his shirt.

"Enough," he muttered.

Max headed into the den in search of Eddie. He turned the corner and stopped in the doorway. The sofa was empty. He continued toward the front room. Soft voices echoed down the hall.

He went to the main room, surprised by the sight of Cassie kneeling beside the computer bloke. She rested her arm on the back of his chair.

"Good morning." Max tried not to sound irritated by the fact that she wouldn't accept his help last night but had obviously awakened Eddie to enlist his service.

Max went to Eddie's desk and slid the mug next to a pile of papers. "Thought you'd need this."

Eddie glanced at the mug. "Thanks, boss."

"I didn't think you'd be awake or I would have poured you something," Max said to Cassie.

She stood, running her hands down her navy slacks, looking rather uncomfortable.

"I'm sorry, did I interrupt something?" Max asked.

"No, no, everything's fine," Cassie said.

Eddie stared at his computer screen.

"Good," Max said. "Why don't you get yourself some coffee?"

She blinked bloodshot eyes at him. "Okay, thanks."

She disappeared around the corner and Max turned his attention to Eddie. He wanted to ask what their little meeting was all about.

"Did you need something, sir?" Eddie glanced up.

"Actually, yes. Did you get that list of e-mails and messages from the latest victim's computer?"

"Yes, sir."

"Good, print them out for me, will you?"

"Yes, sir."

"And Eddie?"

"Sir?"

"Thanks for helping out last night."

"No problem."

Max heard the squeak of someone coming down the hardwood stairs. He turned to see Barnes hesitate at the bottom of the steps, stretching out his neck.

"They'll be down in ten minutes," Barnes said.

The front door swung open and Agent Kreegan walked into the command center, studying a piece of paper in her hand.

"Good morning," Jeremy offered.

"Did you see this?" she said, not looking up. "I found it outside."

It was then that Max noticed she was wearing latex gloves.

"What is it?" Max said.

"Looks like another note from our killer."

Chapter Eight

Jeremy studied the note in the forensics expert's hands. "Where did you find it?"

"Taped to the front door."

"It wasn't out there this morning when I brought in the paper," Jeremy said.

"Which means, not only does he know where we live, but he was here within the last hour." Max opened the front door and stepped outside.

Jeremy watched him glance down the street. Egomaniac killers often enjoyed watching their prey struggle and squirm. He could be standing down the block, waiting for a reaction.

"What's he doing?" Agent Kreegan asked.

"Bag the note and be ready to report," Jeremy said. "Meeting starts as soon as possible."

"Yes, sir." She went to her desk, carefully placing the note in protective plastic.

Jeremy glanced out the front door at Max, who leaned

against the three-foot brick railing. Bobby and Art came down the stairs, Art wearing his usual odd attire: a brown checked suit, white shirt and olive-green tie.

"Coffee is in the kitchen," Barnes said. "We need to get started. There's been a development."

"What's it about, guv?" Bobby asked, rubbing his eyes.

"C.K. dropped off another note."

"Dropped it off?" Art said, astonished.

"Yes. We're meeting in five minutes." Jeremy went out to the front landing, taking a position opposite Max. The former inspector was beating himself up for this, Jeremy could sense it.

Max pushed away from the brick, gripping his cane with deadly force. "Come and get me!" he called out.

With hands braced against the cement rail, Jeremy glanced at his polished shoes, avoiding Max's eyes.

"You think I'm crazy, don't you?" Max said.

Jeremy looked at him. "I think you're frustrated."

"Aren't you?"

"Yes."

"Wouldn't know it by looking at you," Max said.

No, Jeremy was the king of control, always keeping his emotions in order. In his mind, that was the most effective way to function in this profession. And his job was his life.

"I've got to be honest, Barnes."

Jeremy held his breath. Max had never shared anything with him in the past.

"Something doesn't tally." Max leaned against the railing, shaking his head.

"Sir?"

The senior investigator looked at Jeremy. "C.K. never got this close before, never risked it."

"You don't think it's C.K. then?"

"I'm not sure. Either it's someone else, or he's developed an addiction to game-playing he didn't have before."

"Serial murderers do mature," Jeremy offered.

Max started back into the house. "Let's make this quick. I want to get to the fraternity this morning."

"Our appointment is at ten."

"Phone them, push it up."

"Yes, sir."

Jeremy did as ordered, and then joined the team in the front room.

"We're guessing it was dropped off this morning, between six-thirty and seven," Agent Kreegan said. "It wasn't there when Agent Barnes brought in the *Tribune* at six, but I found it taped to the door when I arrived."

"Isn't that rather odd, guv? The killer taking the chance he'd be seen?" Art asked.

"Maybe he hired another messenger," Eddie offered.

"No, he delivered this one himself. It turns him on to get so close," Max said.

"He could also feel shunned because Agent Templeton didn't mention him or the previous murders in the news broadcast," Jeremy said.

"Read the note, Agent Kreegan," Max said.

"'Another boy will fall/ Lose his way/ Lose his life./ You can stop me, Inspector./ But first you have to find me.'"

She glanced up. "That's it."

Max walked to the front window, hesitated and turned to the group. "Quite civil of him to give us a warning. This note seems a little different from the rest."

"Remorse," Jeremy blurted out.

Max glanced at him. "This is a cold-blooded killer we're dealing with."

Jeremy knew that, of course, but sensed something about the note, about the whole process that was different this time around.

The team shared updates and opinions: Agent Kreegan said no prints were found on the latest note; McDonald reported that the family of the second victim said he was upset about grades, but was planning to get a tutor; McDonald said there were no similar murder cases in the past year in the States.

The front door swung open and Spinelli joined the team.

"Am I late?" Spinelli said.

"We needed to get an early start," Jeremy said. "We received another note."

"Hell," Spinelli swore.

"Do you have anything for us?" Max said.

Spinelli settled at a desk and opened his notebook. "I'm checking out a few suspects from the frat house interviews—a plumber who'd done some work there and an advisor who knew both boys. Drew a blank on the scarf—could have been purchased from any number of department stores. There's nothing special about it."

"We need a connection," Max said.

They were running out of time. Max could feel it.

He pushed away from the desk. "Agents Barnes and Kreegan will accompany me to the fraternity this morning for interviews and investigation of the victims' belongings. Agent Spinelli, follow up on the plumber; we'll interview the advisor. We'll meet back here at four o'clock. And a word of advice—we have to be sharp to catch this bastard, which means we need our proper sleep and nourishment."

"That means no cold pizza for breakfast," Cassie said to Eddie.

Max glanced at Bobby. "And let's take it easy on the pub-crawling. If you want to get out and let off steam, fine, but make sure you get your seven hours of sleep, got it?"

Max dismissed the group. Barnes cornered the forensics agent and asked her a question, Art patted Bobby on the shoulder and Bobby shook his head in embarrassment.

"What about me?" Cassie said.

Max glanced at her, taking in her sweet, fair skin, rosy cheeks and bloodshot eyes.

"How about a day off?" he said.

"What if I don't want the day off?"

"I assumed after the night you had that you could use a little time to yourself."

She crossed her arms over her chest. "I don't need you making decisions for me."

He'd made her cross. By caring about her?

"I can't win with you, can I?" he said. It was one thing to be a target of a crazed killer, but he didn't need to be a target of her anger as well. "I was trying to help. I guess that's where I keep making my mistake. Barnes!" he called, and walked away from her.

Barnes looked up from his conversation with Agent Kreegan.

"We'll meet out front in fifteen minutes and head to the fraternity," Max directed.

"Yes, sir. Agent Kreegan wanted you to see this—a report on the substances found in the Cunningham boy's system." Barnes handed him a folder.

"And I've got those e-mails, sir," Eddie said, walking up to him with a handful of papers.

"Thanks." Max took the stack of papers and started up the steps.

A woman's cry pierced his heart. He gritted his teeth and kept climbing, determined not to collapse in full view of the team. He wouldn't allow them to see his post-trauma breakdown.

That cry, a familiar sound, he'd heard it before. The sound of a mother finding her dead son in the rubble at King's Cross.

More like the sound of a mother's anguish after being told her son was brutally murdered by a serial killer.

A killer Max couldn't stop from killing again.

Take me, he thought. *Pick on someone who can fight back.*

And Max would fight, injury be damned, if the bastard would show himself.

"Max?"

He ignored the sound of Cassie's voice. It was all he could do to push aside the spell and get up to his room. He needed a few minutes alone, away from the rush of the investigation.

"What is it?" she said.

She touched his arm but he kept on climbing. He reached the second floor and headed for his room, bracing himself against the wall for support.

"That's it, I'm calling a doctor," she said.

"No, leave me alone." He went into his room and slammed the door.

He leaned against the wall, wondering what had brought on this spell and why he couldn't will it away.

He tossed the file to the bed, his heartbeat hammering against his eardrums. At least the woman's gut-wrenching cry had stopped.

"Sit down."

Cassie. She was there in his room, guiding him to the bed.

"I told you to leave me be." Through the haze he read concern in her eyes.

"Breathe," she said. "Come on, focus on my eyes, stay with me."

He followed her order and stared directly into the light-blue depths that reminded him of the August sky back home: bright, blue, brilliant.

"You're okay," she said.

Something squeezed his right hand, subtly, as if through layers of padding.

"Feel my hand?"

"Yes," he said.

His head cleared a bit. "I'm okay," he said, starting to get up.

"Stay." She pressed her hand to his shoulder. "We need to talk."

Here it comes. Her resignation.

"Your spells," she started.

"It's none of your business."

"I'm making it my business."

"No."

"No? You're going to tell me what I can and cannot do?"

She was giving him a headache.

"No more arguing," he said.

"No arguing, listening. You listen. You want to be able to trust me. Fine. But in order to help you I need to know what's going on. What happens when you have your spells?"

"I get dizzy." He glanced at the floor.

"And?"

"I lose my balance."

"And?"

"And nothing."

She tipped his chin so he'd look into her eyes again.

"Don't," he said.

"What are you afraid of?" she whispered.

"Not finding a killer before he kills again." He stood and walked to the window. His vision cleared, his feet felt like he was on solid ground. The spell had passed, thank God.

"Our problem is we're a lot alike, you and I," he said. "Both of us are too proud to accept help." He turned to her. "Although, you didn't have a problem asking Eddie for help. So it must be me. You don't think I'm up to the task?"

"I didn't ask you for help because I figured you had enough on your plate."

"Right, got it." He looked back out the window.

She came up beside him. "Stop the self-pity crap."

"Out of my way." He started for the door, but she stepped in front of him.

"I asked Eddie to help me find my mother and sisters," she said.

"And you couldn't ask me?"

"You're in charge of a murder investigation, you've got trauma that gives you nightmares and it seems a killer is focused on you." She planted her hands to her hips. "Sorry if I thought I should spare you more angst. I didn't want to put that on you."

"Because I couldn't handle it."

Her eyes burned fire. "No, because I care about you."

She turned to leave, but he caught her arm and pulled her against his chest. As he looked into wide, blue eyes, he lost himself for a second, forgetting where he was and who she was and…

…he kissed her. Just like that. Tasted her sweetness and absorbed her goodness. Her warmth touched a part of him he thought had been destroyed in the blast.

This was wrong, but instead of letting go of her, he let go of his cane. It hit the floor with a thump, and he slipped his hand to the small of her back, pulling her even closer. God, she tasted heavenly.

A knock at the door made them break apart. Max lost his balance, took a step back and sat on the bed. Cassie stared at him, pressing her fingers to her lips.

"What?" Max said to their intruder, keeping his eyes trained to Cassie. She looked…horrified.

"Everything okay, guv?" Bobby asked.

"Fine. I'll be down in a minute."

"Yes, sir."

Cassie leaned against the door, listening to the foot-steps echo down the hallway.

"It seems I'm not the only one who cares," she said.

"But you're the one I kissed." He searched her eyes,

hoping for a sign that she'd welcomed, maybe even enjoyed the impulsive gesture.

Instead, she closed her eyes and sighed.

"I'm sorry," he said.

"Me, too." She opened the door and raced down the hall to her room.

"Now what have you done, Templeton?" he whispered.

FORTY MINUTES LATER, Cassie went into the kitchen of the frat house in search of a glass of water. Max, Jeremy and Agent Kreegan interviewed fraternity brothers in the living room. A campus police officer supervised, along with their college advisor, Gil Jenkins.

She opened a cabinet and found a clean glass. Turning on the water, she heard Max's apology over and over in her head.

I'm sorry.

Although she'd said "Me, too," the truth was, she wasn't sorry. Not about the kiss anyway. It was amazingly tender, and it scared the wits out of her.

She wasn't ready to get involved with a man, especially not a complicated man like Max Templeton who'd surely hurt her with his misplaced pride and unresolved grief.

"You sound like a coward," she muttered.

She took a sip of water and glanced into the backyard. It had all started as a plan to help him work through whatever haunted those brilliant green eyes of his. Eyes that tore at her heart whenever he had a spell.

"I'm surprised you came along."

She turned at the sound of Jeremy's voice.

"Why?" she said. Good heavens, was it that obvious that she'd been rattled by her encounter with Max?

Girl that ain't no ordinary encounter—that was the Fourth of July!

He walked up beside her and glanced out the window. "I don't know. You look tired today. Max said not to wake you. But here you are."

He studied her and she looked away. Jeremy Barnes was an intuitive man, and a gentle one. Some girl would be lucky to have him.

But not Cassie. She wasn't ready for a man, not now, not for a few years.

"I'm okay," she said. "How's it going out there?"

"As well as can be expected. Some of the boys are rattled, others think it's a coincidence."

"What do you think?"

"I think," He hesitated and eyed her. "You're a brave girl."

"Brave? Why?"

"I think you know." Jeremy smiled.

Someone cleared his throat in the doorway. She spun around to find Max standing there.

She automatically took a step away from Jeremy, feeling guilty. *Oh for pity's sake.*

"You're needed upstairs to search the rooms," Max

said, looking at Barnes. "Unless you want to stay here and continue flirting with my assistant."

Jeremy raised a brow and nodded at Cassie, then left the kitchen.

Max hovered in the doorway. "You coming?"

"Of course." She walked across the kitchen.

He placed a hand to her shoulder. "You sure you're up to this?"

When he looked at her with such concern in his eyes it took her breath away. It had been such a long time since a man had cared about her like this. Or had a man ever cared?

Get a grip, girl.

"Let's go." She went through the living room and started up the stairs.

He followed her at a distance. Good. When he got too close she fought the urge to touch him again, reach out and rub her thumb across the faded scar on his cheek. This was bad. Very bad.

Sure, she'd been attracted to Karl at first. But the attraction began to fade, turning into a conscious need for stability and someone to lean on. She'd figured that was the normal evolution of things.

In reality, it was the beginning of a nightmare.

When she looked back on her years with her ex-husband, she realized there had been signs, but she'd chosen to ignore them.

She wasn't ignoring anything about Max. She knew

he was a tortured soul who took out his anger on the people around him. What on earth would compel her to walk into that mess?

His eyes. The glint of hope and promise she saw there. A glint of hope he probably didn't know existed.

Maybe Max was right: maybe she was a sucker for lost causes.

No. Max was far from lost. If he'd only accept his imperfections, and his gifts.

He passed her and went into the bedroom where Jeremy and Agent Kreegan were poking through bookshelves and items on a desk.

Max had many gifts. His keen instinct and loyalty for starters. Then there was his kissing ability...

She couldn't stop thinking about the kiss. And that scared her.

She should leave, hop a plane and fly away from her past and Max. But she couldn't until she helped him through this case, until she helped him accept who he was.

He fingered a notebook on the desk and glanced at her, as if reading her mind.

She crossed her arms over her chest and stared back at him. She was being silly.

"I'll check the TV room," Jeremy said, passing by Cassie and disappearing into the hall.

"This is odd," the forensics expert said. She handed something to Max. It looked like a coin.

With latex-gloved fingers, Max took it from her and went pale.

Cassie casually strode up beside him.

"You all right, sir?" Agent Kreegan asked.

"Fine. Get started in the TV room, will you?"

"Yes, sir." She disappeared into the hallway.

"Max, what's wrong?" Cassie asked.

"I'm fine," he said, a blank look in his eyes.

"No, you're not. Max, look at me. Look into my eyes."

If she could get him to focus, she could bring him back down to earth.

Thundering footsteps echoed up the stairs. "Hey! Somebody, help!" a man shouted.

"What's happened?" Cassie heard Jeremy ask in the hallway.

"Lyle Cooper, no one's seen him since yesterday."

ANOTHER ONE TAKEN and the dream team wasn't even close to finding the mastermind who served up true justice. The boys would fall, one by one, followed by the arrogant Max Templeton. He would fall the hardest. That's what he deserved for getting in the way.

Chapter Nine

Max's gut twisted into a knot. He strode into the hall-way. "Who saw him last?"

"His girlfriend, Beth," a redheaded kid said.

"And you are?"

"Adam, his roommate." He ran his hand through shaggy shoulder-length hair. "I thought he was with Beth last night, so I didn't worry when he never came home. Sometimes he stays at her apartment."

"What time did she leave him?" Barnes asked.

"She had lunch with him around one," Adam said.

The boy wet his lips, twice, three times. He was nervous. Why?

"Lyle told her he had to cram for a physics test, and he'd call to say good-night but he didn't. She figured he was studying so she didn't want to bother him."

"We'll need to talk to her," Barnes said.

"She's downstairs."

"Barnes," Max ordered.

"Yes, sir." Barnes started down the stairs and the boy followed.

"Adam?" Max said, and the boy turned to him. "I'd like a word with you."

"Sure."

Max motioned him into the bedroom. "Continue in the TV room," he ordered Agent Kreegan who had come out into the hall.

"Yes, sir."

She'd found the strange medallion in the boy's bedroom. Maybe she'd get lucky and find another lead.

"Does this look familiar?" Max said, holding up the coin to Adam.

"No, sorry."

Max adjusted himself to lean against the desk. "About your roommate, what was his mood like the past few days?"

"He was a little stressed about his physics test."

"Have you noticed anything unusual?" Max passed the coin to Cassie. "Hanging out with new friends, missing class, odd phone calls?"

"Not really." He shoved his hands into his sweatshirt pockets and licked his lips. Again.

"How long have you known Lyle?"

"Met him last year."

"Were you close?" Max asked.

"Yeah, no, I don't know. Define close."

"Ever party with him?"

The boy's head snapped up and his gaze locked on Max. "Yeah, we went to a few."

Max leveled a stare at him. "Think, boy. Did anything odd happen in the last few weeks? New friends, accidents, chance encounters?"

"No." He studied his shoes.

Max slammed his cane to the floor to get the kid's attention. "Whatever it is you're hiding isn't worth your roommate's life."

Adam clenched his jaw.

"Come on, mate," Max said. "I'm trying to save a boy's life."

Adam sighed. "A few months ago, Lyle went to a party at the beach, without Beth. He didn't come home until eight the next morning. He told me he drank too much and blacked out. Woke up in the back of his car. He couldn't remember what happened."

"Is that typical for him?"

"No, but he and Beth had had a fight, so he went out with some of the guys."

"That's it?"

He licked his lips again. "There was a dent in the front panel of his car. He didn't remember hitting anything. We watched the newspaper, but nothing showed up about a hit and run. Anyway, a few days later Lyle started getting calls from a woman. She'd call, ask to speak with him, and hang up when he'd pick up the phone. She'd always call the house phone, never his cell."

"Same time of day?"

"Yeah, around dinnertime."

"No one recognized her voice?" Max said.

"No."

"You boys thought it was related to what happened at the beach party?"

"Maybe, I don't know." He ran his hand through thick wavy hair.

"Why the guilty conscience?" Max asked.

"I should have stopped him." He looked at Max. "When Lyle drinks it makes him like…somebody else. It's a Jekyll-and-Hyde thing."

"Is it possible he went drinking last night and he's passed out somewhere in the back of his car?" Max asked.

"I doubt it. He wouldn't miss his physics test."

Max sensed there was more to it, that Adam was holding something back.

"Anything else?" Max prompted.

"No." He stood. "I'd better get downstairs. Beth is a mess."

"Cassie, my assistant, will give you our number. If you think of anything else please phone me immediately."

Adam took the card, nodded at Cassie and left.

Agent Kreegan eyed him as he passed her in the doorway. "I'm heading back to the lab to work on the note," she said to Max. "I'll check in later."

"Very good." Max turned his attention to Cassie.

"Phone Eddie, have him get records for incoming calls to the fraternity house for the past two months."

"Yes, sir."

He stepped toward the door. She put her hand to his forearm and he glanced into her eyes. "You okay?"

"Fine, why?"

"You had a strange look on your face before, when you held the coin. I thought, maybe you were having an attack."

"I'm fine." He pulled away from her and they went downstairs.

She knew. She knew his attacks were coming more frequently and with more intensity. What would she do? Tell Barnes? Phone a doctor and have the men in white coats take him away?

No, not before he took care of business and put C.K. behind bars.

"Thank you," Barnes said to the girlfriend, standing and offering her a business card. "Phone us if he contacts you."

In a daze, she took his card. Adam put an arm around her and glanced at Max. It would break her heart to know her missing boyfriend had gone to a beach party and possibly slept with a strange woman, a strange woman who might be his new stalker.

Max asked the college advisor a few questions about the boy's classes and grades. The advisor seemed like a straight-up bloke.

"Thank you." Max shook the advisor's hand.

"If there's anything else we can do to help…"

Max read concern in the advisor's bloodshot eyes. He looked genuinely worried, as if he'd been up all night.

"We'll phone you," Max said.

Max led Cassie and Barnes out the front door.

"What do you make of it?" Barnes said, hesitating on the landing.

"This could be completely unrelated," Max offered. "The boy had an issue with alcohol. He could have gone out last night, consumed a few too many pints and passed out somewhere."

"He had a big test this morning," Cassie reminded him.

He smiled at her. "You're getting to be quite the detective."

She shot him a perturbed look.

"The girlfriend said they had a disagreement," Barnes added.

The three of them started for the car.

"The boy gets in a fight with the girlfriend and goes on a drinking binge? What you women do to us," Max muttered, then looked at Barnes. "The roommate said Lyle went to a beach party a few months ago, got drunk and blacked out. Ever since he's been receiving hangups. I'm going to have Eddie follow up on calls received at the house."

"We should inform the local police," Barnes said. "Maybe he's asleep in his car somewhere and they can find him and put an end to this."

"And there's the coin." He nodded at Cassie and she handed it to Barnes.

"Curious," Barnes said, flipping it over and studying the reverse side. "You think it's important?"

"I do."

"Why?"

"Instinct," Max said.

Barnes narrowed his eyes. "That's it?"

Of course Barnes would challenge him. Barnes was driven by facts and tangibles.

Max opened the car door. "That's it."

Barnes handed the coin back to Cassie and they got into the car, Barnes behind the wheel and Cassie in the back. Max slipped into the passenger seat. That's when he noticed a piece of paper stuck between the wiper blade and the window.

"What, a bloody advertisement?" Barnes muttered, opening his door.

"Barnes!" Max called.

He hesitated and looked at Max.

"Use gloves."

Barnes's irritation turned pensive. He nodded and pulled latex gloves from his jacket pocket. He walked around the front of the car and slipped the note from the windshield wiper blade.

Max knew from Jeremy's expression that it was penned by C.K.

Max swung open his door and went to the sidewalk. He glanced back at Cassie, who'd gone white with the realization that the killer had been dangerously close.

He glanced north, then south. "That cocky sonofabitch."

MAX, CASSIE and Barnes had spent the better part of the morning walking the fraternity neighborhood. They knocked on doors and inquired as to whether neighbors had seen anything strange this morning, whether they'd noticed someone near the team's rented sedan.

No one had seen a thing. It was almost as if C.K. was a ghost.

Once back at the command center, Max passed out copies of the note and read it aloud:

Two boys gone, another taken.
It's right in front of you, clues you've forsaken.
I'll give you another: from blue to red,
Like a copper's uniform, to blood of the dead.
The clock is ticking; two days to go.
I can't help but wonder, why are you so slow?

He paced the front room.

"Spinelli, get back to the fraternity and find me a connection between these boys. Eddie, how are you doing on the phone records from the fraternity?"

"Someone called from the same cell number, same time every day for a little over two weeks. I don't have an ID on the number yet, but I'll get it."

"The bloody e-mails turned up nothing significant," Max said. "Eddie, find out the meaning of the coin we found in Lyle Cooper's room. Cassie, work with him on that, will you?"

Max didn't miss Eddie's puzzled expression that read, why's the coin so important?

Because it was. Max knew it in his chest. Oh, right, like he should be trusting his own instincts, the instincts of a man on the edge?

"Sure," Cassie said. "Oh, and about the Sterling brand of tea, it's mostly sold in the U.S., but you could order it online from another country."

"Fine. Back to forensics—anything on the first note we received this morning?" Max asked.

"No prints," Agent Kreegan said.

"Then move on. Take the note left on the car and analyze every fiber, every spray of ink. There's got to be something here." He glanced at his team. "Thoughts on the new poem?"

"It's more like the original notes from the London murders," Art McDonald said. "He's challenging us—"

"More like mocking us," Bobby said.

Max couldn't believe the arrogance of the killer, nor could he forget the look of fear haunting Cassie's blue eyes. The killer had been too close.

"How did he know we'd be at the fraternity this morning?" Max said, frustration burning low.

He turned to the group. "This is how it works. Agent Spinelli, focus on connections between the victims—habits, classes, interests. McDonald and Finn, contact Lyle Cooper's parents, family members and friends. Get as much as you can on the boy. I'm sure he didn't go off willingly with a serial killer. We need to know where he was last night. If he was stressed about a test, maybe he talked to a family member about it."

He studied the copy of the note he'd been squeezing between his fingers. "What about this clue, 'from blue to red'?"

"From cop to victim," Spinelli offered.

"You think he's a cop? Our killer's a cop?" Eddie said.

"I suppose anything's possible," Max said. "Other theories on the blue to red reference?"

Brainstorming often provoked a new, fresh direction. "There's no wrong answer here," Max prompted.

"Roses are red, violets are blue," Late Eddie offered. "Sorry."

"What else?"

"Christmas red," McDonald said.

"Valentine's Day Massacre," Agent Kreegan added.

"Red rubies," Cassie offered, and shrugged.

"Red beer," Finn said. "Sorry, guv."

"Don't be. Red beer. The boy's roommate said he had

strong reactions to alcohol. What if he had an allergy to wheat in the beer?"

"And he went to a pub to unwind before a big exam," Barnes said. "Drank a pint and it threw him completely off balance."

Amazing how Barnes actually followed Max's train of thought. He snapped his attention away from his second in command. "The color red is the key."

"Red hair," Kreegan said.

"The red light district," Spinelli shot back.

Bobby snorted.

"What?" Spinelli said.

"Wait, that's a thought," Max said. "What if our victims are lured by a beautiful woman?"

"Who wears all red," Bobby added.

"But what's her connection to the killer?" Spinelli asked.

"She's a pawn," Barnes continued for Max. "She's paid a hefty sum to seduce the man, get him alone, and the killer takes it from there."

"But she could identify the killer," McDonald said.

"Not necessarily," Barnes argued. "The whole exchange of money could be anonymous."

"There's a piece missing," Max said. "Red, what's red?"

"The Red Line?" Spinelli offered.

Max turned and stared him down.

"You know, the train?"

"Where does this Red Line travel?" Max asked.

"From 95th and the Dan Ryan up to Howard Street."

"Within blocks of night clubs?"

"Yeah, sure, Rush Street, Lincoln Park."

"Cassie, call the fraternity and get a list of favorite pubs. Eddie, I need pubs along the Red Line train route that would attract college types."

"Why focus on the bars?" Spinelli asked. "The victim wasn't a regular drinker and the red theme could be part of C.K.'s obsession with the color."

"True, it's part of the killer's obsession. I also think drinking could be a contributor to these cases," Max said. "The victim drinks, lets his guard down and the killer preys on his weakness. Alcohol will have passed through the bloodstream by the time the body is found. You have your assignments. Let's get to it."

He went to the window and glanced out onto the calm, peaceful street. Was C.K. out there? Watching him, laughing at him?

Sure he was. He got hard at the sight of Max looking blankly out the window, no closer to finding the killer now than he was yesterday morning.

But that would all change tonight. Max would follow his instinct about the pubs and become the aggressor. God, he hoped his instincts were true and not diseased by the madness infecting his brain.

He turned to call out to Barnes. His gaze caught on Cassie, speaking with Eddie. Had he found her mother and sisters? She hadn't come to Max for help because she didn't want to add to his burden. Max suspected it was something else. Fear. Fear he'd hurt her?

Damn it, man, you've already wounded her by bringing her into this investigation. An investigation that was moving at a snail's pace.

"Barnes?" he said.

"Yes, guv?" Barnes looked up from paperwork on Art McDonald's desk.

"Help them with the list of pubs. We're going clubbing tonight."

THEY'D SPENT the afternoon at the command center researching clues and following up on leads. Cassie put together a list of bars frequented by college students, especially the Sigma Delta Upsilon members, and then she researched the coin. She didn't get very far, so she left it with Eddie.

She'd insisted on accompanying them to the bars. She wanted to be close in case Max had another spell. They hadn't talked about his earlier episode. She wondered if they ever would.

And now, well past nine, she and Max were sitting at Kelsey's, a popular bar in Lincoln Park. Jeremy and Bobby worked the other side of the street.

Max studied the bar, from the mirror-backed shelves displaying bottles of liquor, to the pool tables and big-screen television. She could tell he registered every detail, every nuance.

He motioned for the bartender and placed a photo of Lyle Cooper on the bar. "Did you see this man last night?"

"I was off last night. Mickey was here. He should be here within the hour."

Max nodded, then looked at Cassie. "It's late. You look tired."

"Gee, thanks. Nothing like a compliment to brighten a girl's spirits."

"You didn't have to come," he said.

"But you're glad I did."

"Am I?" He glanced at the front door.

"Does that work for you? That whole denial thing?"

He looked at her through half-closed eyes.

"Yeah, I'm talking to you," she challenged.

He refocused on the door. Was that a wry smile playing at his lips?

"It wouldn't hurt to talk about it," she added.

He glanced at her, raising an eyebrow.

"Right, you're a guy," she said. "Forgot, you don't talk."

"I've got a lot on my mind."

"So to speak," she shot back. It did no good for him to keep it inside. "What happens? Do you have panic attacks or headaches or…?"

He didn't answer. A few minutes passed. She glanced at a couple in the corner, holding hands. She snapped her attention back to a group of men playing pool.

"It started with anger," he said. "I thought it normal from having my life blown apart—" he glanced at her "—literally." He studied patrons in the bar again. "Then I started getting headaches, dizzy spells, sometimes flashbacks. Medications don't seem to help. I hate depending on bloody pills."

"Doesn't surprise me. So, it's officially post-traumatic stress disorder?"

"According to the medical community. As far as I'm concerned, I'm going mad and there's nothing I can do about it."

"I disagree. But you might if you keep avoiding it."

"What do you suggest? I go to group therapy and cry my eyes out?"

"No, but you could start the healing process, deal with the trauma head-on instead of pushing it back."

"Right, and you're the expert, Dr. Clarke?"

"Yeah, actually, I am." She held his gaze, remembering the months of emotional recovery after leaving Karl.

"I'm sorry," he said. "Insensitive of me."

"Hey, I'm used to it," she joked.

"But you shouldn't be. I'm a bastard boss and you should have left me long ago."

"What, and miss out on a free trip to Chicago?"

"Some trip. We're sitting in a pub waiting for nothing. Blast, even my instincts have been affected by this madness."

"I don't think so." She touched his hand. "I may have

been traumatized by Karl's abuse, but I never lost my intuitive skills. You haven't, either."

"No? Then why are we sitting here wasting our time?" He waved a second bartender over. "Did you see this man last night?"

"Ah, I think so."

"Think, or know?"

"I'm not sure, man, sorry. We were packed for the Harry Caray look-alike contest."

"Thanks."

Jeremy and Bobby entered the bar and walked up to Max and Cassie.

"Anything?" Max said.

"No, sir," Jeremy said.

"The bartender *thinks* he saw Lyle Cooper here last night," Max said.

Max knew canvassing the pubs was a long shot, but he'd thought the Red Line train route had been a solid lead, especially when a fraternity brother said Kelsey's was Lyle Cooper's favorite bar.

Another lost day, closer to an innocent boy's death. Max glanced across the pub and something caught his eye—a red light above a door leading into a hallway.

Weakened with drink, lured into a killer's trap.

Instinct drove Max toward the light. Blast, the boy was here last night, Max felt it in his gut.

"What is it, guv?" Bobby asked.

A darkened hallway leading to a back exit: perfect strategy to lure a man into danger.

He pushed open the back door leading outside. Glancing down the long alley lined with trash bins, Max knew that anything could happen in such a remote place. The blaring music of the pubs would drown out any cries for help. But where would C.K. hide the boy for two days?

Barnes's mobile went off.

"Barnes," he answered. He glanced at Max. "We'll be right there." He snapped his phone shut. "Agent Kreegan was just assaulted outside the command center."

Chapter Ten

Agent Ruth Kreegan recited the event with calm professionalism. Max listened, trying to ignore her red cheek and the lost expression in her eyes.

He felt responsible for this attack as sure as if he'd been the attacker. Max should have known that if the bastard was bold enough to walk up to the building and leave a love note, he wouldn't hesitate to go after a team member.

But why? Were they getting close?

"He popped out from the shadows?" Barnes asked.

Max kept his distance, and his mouth shut. He feared the vile curses that would escape his lips.

"I didn't see anything." She glanced at Max, her eyes grayed and tired. "I had no clue he'd come after me."

Of course not. She was a laboratory creature, a scientist who solved cases from fingerprints and DNA. He read disappointment in her eyes, disappointment that he'd been unable to protect her from the savagery.

"The killer has never gotten this close before," Art said.

"Why attack her, guv?" Bobby asked.

The front door burst open. Spinelli came into the kitchen. "I came as soon as I heard. What the hell happened?"

"She must be close to something vital," Barnes said.

"Or he's trying to spook us," Bobby added. "Letting us know how close he is."

"Coward," Spinelli offered, standing straight. "He should try picking on someone his own size."

Max glanced at Agent Kreegan, then at Cassie. She stood in the doorway, arms crossed over her chest, as if trying to steel herself from the trauma. Would the killer attack another member of his team? Keep going after the weak links: Agent Kreegan, the computer geek, maybe even Cassie?

"I'm sorry I didn't get a good look at him," Agent Kreegan said, her voice cracking.

Cassie sat next to her at the table and held an ice pack to the woman's cheek. "You'll want to hold this here to keep the swelling down."

Cassie probably thought she'd seen the last of this kind of violence, yet here she was, back in the thick of it.

Because of Max.

"Spinelli, take Agent Kreegan home," Max ordered. "Be careful you're not followed."

"Come on, Ruth," Spinelli said, offering her his hand.

Agent Kreegan stood, glanced at Max and said, "Sorry."

"Nonsense. There's nothing to be sorry about."

"This is why I came back." She pulled a folder from her briefcase and placed it on the table. "My analysis of the note left on the car this morning. No prints, but the paper is unusual. I was hoping Eddie could trace it."

"I'll get right on it," Eddie said, grabbing the folder, and disappearing down the hall.

"Don't forget this." Cassie handed Agent Kreegan the ice pack.

"Thanks," Kreegan said, and shuffled out with Spinelli by her side.

"What do you think, guv?" McDonald asked.

"Not sure," Max said. "Could you finish up the last two pubs? Run the photograph past the bartenders and see if anyone recognizes the Cooper boy. We think he stopped into Kelsey's last night. Maybe he popped into another pub as well."

"Yes, sir."

"Bobby, keep working on background about Lyle Cooper."

"On it, guv."

"Barnes, join me upstairs for a minute?" Max said.

Max brushed past Cassie, not making eye contact. He couldn't bring himself to see the look of disillusionment in her eyes after he made his next move.

He had no choice. He was putting his team in danger. Between his unstable mental condition and the killer's personal vendetta, it had become obvious in the last hour what he had to do. He had to remove himself from Blackwell—for everyone's benefit.

He climbed the stairs to the second floor and went into the TV room. Barnes followed.

"Close the door, will you?" Max said.

Barnes closed the double glass doors and turned to him, question in his eyes.

"You and the Patron of Blackwell were wrong to bring me onto this case," Max started. "I think it's best that I leave tomorrow."

"You're not serious."

Max clenched his jaw.

"What's this about?" Barnes asked.

"It's about me endangering the lives of the people on this team. C.K. is trying to undermine our investigation by destroying me, and what better way than to go after my team? He knows how protective I am of all of you."

"Except me."

"Don't joke about this, Barnes. Agent Kreegan could have been killed."

"She knew the risks when she joined the team."

"She didn't know this kind of thing could happen." Max paced to the window.

"This isn't your fault."

"The bloody hell it isn't." The inability to catch the killer before he hurt the people around him tore him up inside.

"We're only two days into this case and you're giving

up already? What about the dead boys? What about Lyle Cooper?"

"You'll find him."

"Not without your help."

"Rubbish." He turned to glare at him. "I didn't want this assignment. You came looking for me, remember? Foolish on your part. I'm wondering if Charles Edmonds was right, that I'm not as good as my reputation. It's obvious I'm not up to solving this case." He eyed Barnes. "You suspected as much, didn't you? But you were trying to ease your guilty conscience by making me the lead and giving me another chance."

Barnes narrowed his eyes, only slightly. God, the man was a rock of control.

"There isn't a day that goes by that I don't feel guilty about what happened at King's Cross," Barnes said, his voice low. "But I won't take the blame for you being a coward."

All the rage, all the frustration of the past year shot to the surface. Max slugged Barnes in the jaw, biting down at the pain shooting through his knuckles. Barnes stumbled back and Max started for the door.

"Don't you walk away from this," Barnes said.

He grabbed Max from behind and pinned him against the wall. Max jerked his elbow back, nailing Barnes in the ribs. Barnes released him and Max spun around.

"Have you gone mad?" Max said, horrified by the man's bloody lip.

But instead of answering him, Barnes lunged.

They tumbled to the floor, each trying to pin the other. Adrenaline shot to every nerve ending of his body, blowing any rational thought from his mind. The bombing…his resignation…the headaches and dizzy spells…hiding out in Seattle…Cassie.

A sweet girl he may very well have put in danger by bringing her here.

Heartbeat pounding in his ears, Max pushed off his second in command.

"Enough," Max said, standing. Using his cane for balance, he leaned over, grabbed Barnes's glasses from the floor and offered them to him.

Barnes's lip was swollen and blood dripped from his nose. Max's gut twisted into knots.

Like an athlete, Barnes got up and took the glasses from Max.

"Glad we finally got that out of the way," Barnes said, brushing his lenses with his shirttail. The crisp white shirt had been pulled from his pants during the row. He nodded at Max, as if they'd just finished a civilized business meeting. Barnes glanced behind Max and his eyes widened.

Max turned to find Cassie standing in the doorway; her eyes round as saucers.

Shame tore at his chest. Without a word, he brushed past her and went down the hall. He had to get away, get some air.

Get his bloody perspective.

"Blast it, Barnes," he muttered.

He swung open the door to the fire escape and looked up at the Chicago night sky. Then he glanced at his hands: blood smears colored them; the color of death.

Another boy would die because of Max's incompetence, and he was wasting time brawling with his own man.

"Bloody hell!"

He'd truly gone mad.

"Let me help," Cassie said.

"I can manage." Jeremy dabbed at his nose with a cold washcloth. He eyed himself in the bathroom mirror: his nose bled but wasn't broken, his lip was going to be swollen by morning.

He'd do the same thing over again to challenge Max's conscience. Jeremy knew if Max left now, he'd never forgive himself.

Jeremy wouldn't allow that. The man had suffered enough.

"What happened?" Cassie said.

Jeremy eyed her in the mirror. He'd always suspected she was a lot tougher than Max realized.

"Disagreement," Jeremy said, inspecting his nose.

"I'll get you some ice."

"I'm fine. It's Max who needs your help."

"He didn't look so bad."

Jeremy eyed her.

"I mean, not that you didn't get your licks in, I'm sure you did."

"His injuries go a lot deeper than a bloody lip," Jeremy said.

"Can you tell me what started the fight?"

"He's threatening to leave."

"Why?"

"He's blaming himself for the attack on Agent Kreegan."

"That's nonsense."

Jeremy ran the washcloth under cold water. "Blame is a powerful emotion. I was hoping to change his mind before he drowned in it."

"Did you?"

He placed the washcloth in the sink and looked at her. "I think so. Can't be positive. Maybe you should have a go at it."

She fiddled with the gold locket around her neck. "I don't think he wants to see me right now. I could tell by the look on his face he's ashamed of himself."

"Well, he shouldn't be. I intentionally provoked him." He went back to tending his lip. "I'll do anything to get him back in the fight. He's spent the last year loafing around feeling sorry for himself. He's better than that."

"You really care about him," she murmured.

She looked at him as if trying to make out his character. Jeremy avoided eye contact. She was dangerous, this little blonde. She had a way of looking past Jeremy's well-practiced composure and into the angst buried deep inside. He also sensed she was a master of compassion, something that mystified Jeremy.

Her compassionate nature made her perfect for Max.

"Go on," Jeremy said, looking into the mirror and holding her gaze. "Help him."

Cassie smiled and touched his shoulder. He held perfectly still, totally unaffected by her gesture. If Cassie didn't know better, she'd think him cold and detached.

"I'll get slugger some ice." She turned and walked down the hall, framing her cheeks with her hands.

She made her way down to the kitchen and filled a towel with ice. The reality was, Max needed a lot more than ice: he needed understanding—and someone to challenge him out of his darkness.

Forging upstairs to the fire escape, she went in search of her patient. Struggling with a loose rung, she awkwardly climbed the ladder, figuring this is where she'd go if she needed to hide out and escape her own shame.

She suspected Max felt ashamed for losing it with Jeremy. She'd read it in his eyes.

Making her way to the roof, she squinted to see into the darkness. The half-moon only slightly lit the roof. "Max?"

No response.

"Come on, where are you? It's creepy up here."

"Then go back down," his deep voice said.

She spotted him, sitting down, leaning against the wall.

She took a deep, calming breath and brought him the ice pack, praying for courage to say the right thing. Lord knows having Max in her life had forced her to be strong. And it had allowed her to feel compassion for a man—a first since Karl's abuse.

"I brought you some ice," she said, standing over him.

"I don't need it."

"Ah, tough guy, huh?"

"More like madman." He looked up at her with that lost expression. Blood smeared across his lip.

"Looks like Jeremy got his licks in." She kneeled beside him and pressed the ice to his lip. "Tell me you didn't rip the stitches from your hand."

"I didn't." He watched her.

She kept her eyes trained to the ice pack.

"You shouldn't be here," he said.

"Hey, it's nice on the roof. Why should you be the only one to enjoy the view?" She studied the stars.

She felt the warmth of his hand touch hers. She glanced at him. His expression of shame mixed with regret tugged at her heart.

"You really should leave me alone," he said.

"Why? So you can beat yourself up?"

"I'd rather it be me than you." He took the ice from her and dropped it beside him. "You saw me down there, you saw what I did to one of my own men."

"It sounds like the two of you had been working up to that for a long time."

"I'm unstable."

"You don't believe that. I know you don't. You feel responsible for the attack on Agent Kreegan. I understand that. You're a perfectionist."

"How did you get that from me threatening to leave the team and beating up Barnes?"

"First, Barnes provoked you on purpose. He admitted as much. Second, I know you're down on yourself for not finding the killer yet. It's been two days, Max. No one's that good."

"I should leave. I'm putting my people in danger by being here."

"No, actually, you're punishing yourself because one of your agents was attacked."

"And I was helpless to prevent it. Just like…"

"Just like what? The bombing?" She sat back on her heels. "Man, you've got an ego the size of Texas."

"Come again?"

"You think you're some kind of superhero who can save a station full of civilians single-handedly, or find a serial killer in forty-eight hours? Get over yourself. Accept yourself for who you are and move on."

"And who is that, exactly?"

"A very smart detective who's got a little extra something going for him."

"What, my good looks?" he joked.

"That, and your keen investigative skills."

With a set jaw, he glanced at his hands.

"Did it ever occur to you that your post-trauma condition may have heightened your sensitivity to things, sharpened your instinct? It's possible. But you've got to deal with this head-on instead of running from it."

He shot to his feet. "The only thing to deal with is my inability to find a kidnapped college student. Blast, it's as if the killer is always two steps ahead of us, like he knows our next move."

"You sent Agent McDonald back to the bars," she said. "Something will turn up."

"And if we don't find him?"

"It's not your fault," she said.

"The bloody hell it isn't."

"Hey, guv?" Bobby said from the fire escape. "The Cooper boy's been found."

Chapter Eleven

Max leaned into his cane; regret tearing at his soul. No, the team still had twenty-four hours to find the boy.

"Where?" he said.

"He's at Northwestern Hospital."

"He's…"

"Alive," Bobby said.

Tension drained from Max's body. "Where did they find him?"

"In an alley a few blocks from Kelsey's. Come downstairs, guv, and we'll fill you in."

Bobby disappeared from view.

Max took a deep breath and glanced to the heavens in a silent prayer of thanks.

Lyle Cooper was alive. Max hadn't failed. Yet.

"You okay?" Cassie touched his arm.

"Better than I was five minutes ago." He started for the ladder. "This isn't over. He'll take another boy and we'll be back to fumbling around in the dark."

"Max." She placed her hand to his arm.

He stopped and glanced at her.

"He was found only blocks from where we were tonight." She smiled and withdrew her hand. "We must have been very close."

He hooked his cane to his forearm and climbed down the ladder, needing to get away from her. He didn't want to continue the conversation about his growing madness. Maybe she was right, maybe facing it head-on would finally be the end of it.

But would he ever be able to let go of the anger, fueled by incredible guilt?

He stepped off the ladder and waited for her. Reaching up to steady her, Max grabbed her waist. The scent of mango taunted him, challenging him to rub his lips against her fine blond hair. She pulled away and turned to face him.

Had she caught him fighting his attraction?

Without warning she placed her hand to his cheek. "It's okay."

No, it wasn't. If it were truly okay, they would have found C.K. by now. They would be heading back to Seattle where he'd help her find another job, away from Max. She deserved better. She deserved a whole, stable man.

He couldn't breathe with her touching him like this, so tender, so gentle, as though she wanted to heal him somehow. He grabbed her wrist and slid her hand from his face.

"We need to get downstairs." He ripped his gaze

from her questioning blue eyes, innocent eyes that held such promise for something he knew could never be.

He opened the door and motioned for her to lead the way, quite proud of himself for resisting the urge to kiss her again.

He kept a safe distance as they went downstairs. He couldn't risk getting that close again, close enough for her to set his cheek aflame with the touch of her hand.

A proper gentleman would put her on a plane tomorrow before he lost all sense and self-control. Besides, he knew this case was far from over. If C.K. had lost control of his victim, he'd be more determined to make the next one pay with his life.

They entered the front room of the command center.

"Let's have it," Max said.

Bobby straightened and read from his notebook. "Lyle Cooper was found fumbling about in the alley behind the Red Lion Pub. The victim was disoriented, muttering, bumping into walls, that sort of thing. A bartender phoned police, who ordered an ambulance. The boy had contusions on his head, scratches on his arms."

"We need to interview him," Max said.

"Hospital staff said no visitors until morning." He glanced at Max. "I've got a theory, guv. I think our canvass of the neighborhood messed up C.K.'s plans, he lost control of the situation and Lyle Cooper escaped." Bobby glanced at the doorway. "You look bloody awful."

Max turned to see Barnes, arms crossed over his chest as if he hadn't a scratch or bruise on him. Truth was, he looked like he'd gone five rounds in a boxing ring.

More like one round with a madman.

"You should see the other guy," Barnes joked.

"We need someone to keep watch over the Cooper boy," Max said, directing the focus back to the investigation. "Barnes, call Spinelli. Have him swing by the hospital after he drops off Kreegan. Since the Cooper boy has turned up, phone McDonald and have him return from the pubs. You and I will interview the Cooper boy tomorrow." Max snapped his attention away from Barnes. "Seems we have a temporary reprieve. I have a feeling C.K. is going to step things up next time around. We'd all better get a good night's sleep."

Max noticed Late Eddie motion to Cassie. He must have uncovered information about Cassie's mother and sisters. A part of Max wished he could be the one to help her reunite with her family.

It was better this way: better that she depend on someone like Eddie the computer geek than on a dangerous and unstable sod like Max.

He brushed past Barnes and made for the stairs, needing time to process today's events.

"Guv?" Barnes followed Max. "Does this mean you're staying on?"

"Looks that way." He hesitated at the top of the stairs.

Barnes stepped up beside him.

"You should put some ice on that." Max motioned to his swollen lip.

"You almost sound like you care." Barnes cracked a half smile.

"Don't count on it." Max went to his room and shut the door, needing time alone, time to think and get his bearings back. He paced to the window and cracked it open, fully intending to light up. Then he realized it had been days since he'd smoked, and he hadn't even missed it, his mind so absorbed in finding a killer.

A killer who had either screwed up or had planned the boy's escape to further engage the team in his game of torture and death.

No, C.K. had screwed up. What had Bobby said? That the team's presence had thrown the killer off and contributed to the boy's escape?

"Wishful thinking, mate," he whispered.

If he accepted that, he'd have to consider the possibility that Cassie was right: Max's post-traumatic stress had heightened his sensitivity and sharpened his instinct, instinct that had led them close to the killer.

Now he truly sounded mad.

ANTICIPATION kept Cassie awake well past midnight. She tried counting sheep, pigs and whales. She even tried reading a mystery she'd found on the shelves. Nothing worked.

She put the book down and slipped the piece of paper out of her sweatpants pocket.

Eddie had located her mother.

She ran her finger across the address: 145 Cleveland Street, Elgin. Her mother had relocated to the western suburbs. According to the report, the Des Plaines house had been sold last year. Mom had signed the documents using her maiden name, which meant she must have finally gotten a divorce.

Could Cassie do this, show up out of the blue on her mom's doorstep? Would she embrace her daughter, or would she be ashamed of the young woman for marrying an abuser, then abandoning her mother and her sisters?

She tried picturing herself visiting Mom's new house, ringing the doorbell, seeing her face. But Cassie wasn't alone. In the picture, Max stood by her side.

"Not good," she muttered.

He was becoming a part of her life, a good friend, no, more than that. She was starting to care about him, a lot.

She needed him.

Her worst fear. Needing him meant she'd grown to depend on him. She'd never make that mistake again. She was safe on her own, independent.

And safety was key for Cassie.

A muffled sound snapped her attention away from the note. She placed it back in her pocket and swung the covers off. Surely everyone had to be asleep at this time of night. She glanced at her clock radio. One-fifteen.

She climbed out of bed and opened her door. She waited. Maybe it was her imagination.

She was about to close her door when she heard it again: the sound of a man crying out.

"Max," she whispered. She grabbed her robe from the chair and headed down the hall to his room. The nightmares were terrifying. She knew that better than anyone.

She knocked softly on his door. "Max?"

Another door opened down the hall. Jeremy stuck his head out of his bedroom.

Max cried out again. She placed her hand to his doorknob hoping he hadn't locked it. She glanced at Jeremy, who shot her an understanding nod, and closed his door.

She went into Max's room. He'd left a desk lamp on; to chase away the demons? She'd slept with a light on for months after she'd moved to Seattle.

"Max?" she said, touching his bare shoulder.

His sheets were strewn across the bed; his pack of cigarettes had been knocked to the floor.

"Wake up," she said.

His eyes shot open, glassy and wide. "I can't get to him. I can see him, but I can't get to him."

"It's okay now," she hushed him, shifting onto the bed and resting his head in her lap. She stroked his thick, black hair, remembering how desperately she'd needed someone to hold her a year ago, hold her and tell her everything was going to be okay.

"Relax," she said. "We'll find him."

She leaned against the headboard and stroked his hair until his breathing slowed. His white-knuckled fingers balled the cotton fabric of her robe.

Max was used to being strong and in charge. But between the stress of this murder case, and battling post-traumatic stress, he must feel completely out of control.

A terrifying feeling.

"Got to stop it… Blood everywhere…" he muttered, with a catch in his breath.

She wondered if he was dreaming about this case or the bombing that had changed his life.

"It's okay, Max. Everything's okay," she whispered, stroking his hair, hoping her touch would ground him. Her other hand trailed down his bare shoulder. She noticed an ugly scar across his lower back. God he must have gone through hell after the bombing.

His breathing slowed and his fingers relaxed their grip on her robe.

"It will be fine," she said, knowing that in the end what mattered most was your attitude about your situation.

She'd taken a horrible situation and had turned it around, made a new life for herself. Now if she could only help Max do the same.

A SHARP KNOCK jolted Max from a deep sleep. Good God, he couldn't remember the last time he'd slept so soundly.

"Meeting in twenty minutes!" Barnes called through the door.

Max glanced at the door, then at the woman lying beside him.

Cassie.

What in the bloody hell was she doing here?

He noticed his hand resting protectively on her hip. He snatched it back and got out of bed, standing there for a good ten seconds, trying to figure out what to do. He needed a bloody smoke, but he'd left them on the nightstand on her side of the bed.

She rolled onto her back and sighed, then opened her eyes.

"Hey, how'd you sleep?" She smiled at him.

The room tipped sideways.

"You're in my bed." *Brilliant, mate.*

She sat up and stretched her arms over her head. She acted as though sleeping next to him was a completely normal affair, like…she'd been completely satisfied by a long night of pleasurable lovemaking.

"You had a nightmare," she said.

"I did not," he said. Good God, had she heard him all the way down the hall and come to his rescue?

"Okay, *I* had a nightmare." She smiled again.

He couldn't move. He stood there, like a complete idiot, in nothing but his undershorts.

She yawned. "What time is it?" She glanced at the clock. "Crap! We're going to be late."

She threw off the covers and whipped open the door. "See you downstairs!" she said over her shoulder and disappeared.

Yes, he surely would see her. He snatched the pack of cigarettes from the floor, his hip aching in protest. Bugger, this had become bloody awkward.

Now why's that, mate? It's not like you made love to the girl.

But he wished he had.

Bad, very bad. This was a professional relationship. Besides, this woman was too fragile to be stuck with Max's mental issues. He glanced at the bed where he'd been snuggled up against her warm body, his hands all over her.

The girl was recovering from trauma of her own and he'd used her as a security blanket. He should be ashamed of himself.

Yet a part of him welcomed the good night's sleep. He glanced at the clock. Great, he had fifteen minutes to get downstairs. Didn't look good if the team's leader was late.

In record time he showered and shaved, threw on clothes and made it downstairs. Coffee, he needed coffee.

A few team members were already at their desks, going over notes and waiting for the day's assignments. Max headed for the kitchen where Barnes poured hot water into a mug. Art stood beside him.

Art glanced up. "Hey, guv, how'd you sleep last night?"

Barnes, whose room was near Max's, smiled slightly

as he stared into his cup. Did he know about Cassie's middle-of-the-night visit?

"I slept fine," Max said. "Why do you ask?"

"I tossed and turned all night. Can't get used to the humidity."

Barnes stepped out of the way and Max poured himself coffee.

"I'll meet you inside." Art headed for the front room.

Barnes followed him.

"Jeremy?" Max said.

"Yeah, guv?"

He wanted to say, "Sorry for beating the tar out of you." Instead, he squeezed the mug between his fingers.

"I don't know about you, guv, but I'm frustrated as hell," Jeremy said. "C.K. has never anticipated our approach before. It's almost like he's a step ahead of us, stringing us along."

"Then the trick is to get three steps ahead of him, yeah?"

"Yes, sir." Barnes turned and disappeared down the hall.

Max started for the meeting and passed Cassie in the hallway. She looked bright and cheerful this morning, her hair pulled back with a headband, her smile full and genuine.

"Coffee's on," he said. "Not as good as yours, but it should do the trick."

"Thanks, Max." She sauntered into the kitchen.

She'd called him Max. Well, that was a first. Sure,

why not? She'd spent the night holding him while he sobbed in her arms. After that kind of intimacy you tend to drop formalities.

Max went to the front of the room. "Where's Agent Kreegan?"

"Had a problem with her daughter," Jeremy said. "She's on her way."

"Right. Listen up, Agent Barnes and I will visit the hospital and interview the victim. Agent McDonald, anything from the pubs last night?"

"Dead end, guv," McDonald said. "But I'm following up on a few leads I picked up from speaking with the Cooper boy's brother."

"What else?" Max prompted, glancing at his team.

"The plumber was a dead end," Eddie said. "Spinelli had me check him out. Records confirm that the guy was out of town during the first murder and he had an alibi for the second. Nothing suspicious about the college advisor, either. He's happily married, volunteers at the YMCA and is on various boards of charitable organizations. He's a stand-up guy."

"Aren't they all?" McDonald muttered.

"What else?"

"I've got something on the coin," Eddie offered. "If you look through a magnifying glass you can make out Themis, the Goddess of Justice."

"Lyle Cooper was pre-law so that makes sense," Barnes said.

Still, something nagged at Max's brain. *Keep moving, mate.*

"Eddie, see if you can find security video from the pubs in the immediate area of where the boy was found," Max said. "Agent Barnes will get you the names and contact information for those pubs. Agent Barnes, did you speak with the Cooper family?"

"Yes, guv. We have their permission to interview the boy."

"Excellent. Agent Finn will accompany us to the hospital to relieve Spinelli. The good news is we no longer have the time pressure to contend with. That said, let's find C.K. before he snatches another victim. Check in at four."

He spotted Cassie in the hallway, reaching up to touch Barnes's swollen lip. That was her way, to heal and comfort. That's what last night was about. She'd heard Max screaming in his sleep and had come to his rescue.

That's when he admitted something quite frightening: he wished she'd come into his room because she wanted him. He wished she were attracted to him as a man, not as a casualty of war needing triage.

The truth was, he'd grown attached to her, not for her secretarial skills, but he'd grown attached to her refreshing smile and sassy mouth. Nothing scared her off, not even a broken man with a chip on his shoulder the size of Great Britain.

This can go nowhere.

Hadn't that kiss proved otherwise?

Finn waited in the hallway with Barnes and Cassie. Max walked up to them, cupping Cassie's elbow. "Why don't you stay back and relax today?"

"What if I don't want to relax?"

Barnes and Finn looked terribly uncomfortable, as if they were eavesdropping on a marital squabble.

"I'll meet you outside," Max said to them.

He redirected his attention to Cassie. "We could be sitting at the hospital for hours waiting for the boy to wake up. Surely you've got better things to do with your time."

"What's that supposed to mean?"

"Eddie found your mum, didn't he?"

"Yes."

"Take the day and go see her. I don't need you."

The four words felt strange coming out of his mouth, and her expression looked even stranger, as if he'd insulted her somehow.

"I'd rather not go alone," she said.

"Fine. When we solve this case, you can take someone from the team with you. Eddie's good company, or maybe Barnes? He's a solid chap."

She shook her head.

"What?"

"For a detective, you can be so obtuse." She brushed past him and went out the front door.

Now what had he done? He was trying to be helpful, show the same concern and compassion that she showed him last night.

He'd never understand women, and now wasn't the time to try. He followed her to the rented SUV. She climbed into the back with Bobby, chatting away as though they were old friends. Max got into the front beside Jeremy.

They pulled away from the curb and Jeremy navigated city traffic like a pro.

"Nice job for someone used to driving on the other side of the road," Max said.

"You'll find I'm full of surprises."

That smart-aleck tone that used to irk Max now entertained him. Maybe he'd pegged Jeremy all wrong from the start. Sure, the man had wanted his job at SCI, but he wouldn't have wished Max harm.

Max thought about their row last night, how Barnes had challenged him. It was almost as if Barnes was trying to help Max move on. And help himself as well.

Max looked at him. "It wasn't your fault."

Cassie and Bobby quieted.

"I'm sorry?" Barnes said, glancing at Max, then back at traffic.

"You aren't responsible for my disability. I was in the wrong place at the wrong time."

"Because of me," Jeremy said, his voice flat.

"No, because of something neither of us could control." He paused. "Fate."

"I don't believe in fate."

"No." He studied Jeremy. "I don't suppose you would."

Max, on the other hand, had started to believe in many things he wouldn't have a month ago: unconditional compassion from a sweet girl, the possibility of finally putting C.K. in prison, and yes, maybe even finally healing from post-trauma madness.

Was Cassie right? Had the condition heightened his sensitivity to other things as well, sharpening his instinct?

The coin still puzzled him, yet he wasn't sure why. Themis, the Goddess of Justice, a coin that Lyle Cooper's roommate did not recognize. Since he lived with Cooper, wouldn't he have noticed the coin around—on a desk, on the boy's dresser?

Cassie had challenged Max to accept who he was and move on. A part of him wanted to give up his rage at having his identity stripped from him in the bombing. But in a way, it had kept him alive these past ten months. At least he could feel something, even if it was the burn of anger.

They made the rest of the drive in relative silence, only a few murmurs issuing from the back seat as Cassie pointed out various Chicago sights.

Too bad they weren't visiting under better circumstances. He'd love to see the sights through her eyes.

She was a giving person, and she needed someone with a mundane career, not someone whose life's work was chasing down the vilest of criminals. Max couldn't start a barbecue fire, but he could pick a criminal out of a lineup with eighty percent accuracy.

Cassie had experienced plenty of personal violence in her life. She needed a man who could take her away from all that, a man who would cherish her and offer her an unremarkable life filled with children and annual family holidays.

They parked in the hospital garage and started for the elevator. Jeremy's mobile went off.

"Barnes," he answered and slowed his pace. "But we were just there."

He stopped short of the elevator. "We'll send someone back straight away." He flipped his mobile closed. "Someone broke into the command center."

"But how is that possible? McDonald and Eddie were there," Max said, panicked. To think he'd almost left Cassie behind.

"McDonald went to get breakfast," Barnes said. "When he returned the place was ransacked and Eddie was gone."

Chapter Twelve

"Missing?" Cassie said.

Max wanted to wipe the fear from her eyes.

Get focused, he scolded himself.

"Barnes, go back to the house," Max said. "Bobby, you'll stay with the Cooper boy as planned. I'll conduct the interview and we will catch a cab back."

"Yes, sir." Barnes started toward the car.

"Don't assume the worst," Max added. "Eddie could have gone after the intruder."

Knowing the kid's enthusiasm, he probably did. Max, Bobby and Cassie took the lift to the sixth floor. He noticed she rubbed her locket.

He placed a comforting hand to her shoulder. "I'm sure he's all right."

She shot him a tentative smile.

Truth was, Max wasn't sure of anything, except for his need to keep her close. This case was getting more strange with every turn: a victim getting away, his own people being assaulted by the killer, and now the command center being broken into and an agent gone missing.

He hoped Lyle Cooper remembered something that would give them a fresh start. They stepped off the lift and headed for the boy's hospital room.

He spotted Spinelli sitting outside a room down the hallway.

"Good morning," Max greeted.

"Good morning, sir. Chicago PD just left. Said we could interview the boy."

"Excellent. You're relieved of duty. Bobby will take over. Get a few hours sleep and meet us back at the command center."

"I dozed last night, sir. I'm fine."

"Very good. Someone broke into the command center and Eddie's gone missing. Head back there and help Barnes."

"Yes, sir."

Max went into the hospital room, Cassie and Bobby trailing close behind. Max approached the boy's bed. "How are you, Mr. Cooper?" He had a few lacerations on his face, a goose egg on his forehead and an IV inserted into his hand.

"Who are you?" the boy asked.

"Max Templeton, lead agent for the Blackwell Group. We investigate violent crimes like kidnapping, murder, that sort of thing."

"You're the guy who found me?" He sat a little straighter.

"No, that was a bartender," Max explained.

"He called for help, but you found me."

Max's blood ran cold. "Sorry?"

"The guy who kidnapped me said your name. Over and over, he kept saying, 'How did Templeton find me?'"

Max took a deep breath and leaned against the wall for support. He *had* been close last night.

"Let's start from the top. We know you had lunch with your girlfriend yesterday. What happened after that?"

Cassie pulled out her notebook and pen.

"I went to the library to study for my physics test. A few hours go by and I get a call from some woman saying Beth is at Kelsey's, drunk out of her mind. It doesn't make sense because she rarely drinks. I rush over to the bar but I can't find her. I ask the bartender and he says a woman left a note. All the note says is, Out back. So I go into the alley and I call her name."

"Did you see anyone?" Max asked.

"No, but I heard a woman whimpering. I turned to see where it was coming from and I got stung, by a bee, I guess. I'm allergic so I thought I was a goner. Then I heard this weird voice, not human. And I'm drifting down the alley, into a room. I don't know." He waved his hand. "Maybe I was hallucinating."

"Why do you say that?" Max asked.

"Because I remember weird stuff—someone wearing

a Mardi Gras mask, talking in a weird voice. I heard a woman singing. It doesn't make sense."

"What else do you remember?"

"I don't know. I think I passed out. When I woke up the Mardi Gras guy was pacing the room. That's when he mentioned your name." He looked at Max. "The guy was freaking out. My wrists were tied together, but I managed to get up, push him out of the way and run outside. That's the last thing I remember." He pinned Max with teary, bloodshot eyes. "Why did this happen to me?"

"That's what we're going to find out. In the meantime, may I have your permission to leave Agent Finn for your protection until your parents arrive?"

"Sure."

"Mr. Cooper, can you think of any connection between you, Michael Cunningham and Peter Stanton?" Max said.

Lyle Cooper glanced at the IV in his left hand. "No. Other than being fraternity brothers, I really can't."

"And what about the crank calls you were getting?"

His gaze shot up. "You know about that?"

"It helps us to know as much as possible."

"The calls stopped about a week ago. I don't know why. I think it was a girl I'd met at a party a few months ago. I'd had too much to drink and ended up with her." He glanced at Max. "I'm not proud of that fact."

"Do you know her name?" Max asked.

"Cheryl, I think. Yeah, Cheryl."

"Last name?"

"No, sorry. I only saw her that one time. I don't think she went to Jamison."

"I'll let you get some sleep."

"Thanks." Lyle closed his eyes and turned onto his side.

Max motioned for Bobby to follow him into the hallway. Cassie joined them.

"Bobby, I need you to get close to the boy. Make him feel like you're his best friend."

"Guv?"

Max glanced into Lyle Cooper's hospital room. "I think he's holding something back." He looked at Bobby. "Earn his trust. Check in later."

"Sure, guv."

Max led Cassie to the lift.

"You think the Cooper boy is lying?" Cassie whispered. "Come on, you saw his injuries."

"I don't think he's lying about the abduction. But he's leaving something out."

"How do you know?"

He smiled. "Instinct. He's keeping something from us. Maybe not intentionally, but it could be the key to finding the killer."

THE CHAOTIC SCENE at the house stunned Cassie. Papers were scattered everywhere, chairs were tipped onto their sides, and a few computers were strewn on the floor. She eyed Eddie's desk. His laptop looked as though someone had smashed it with a hammer. She started to feel relief that he'd found her mother before his equipment had been destroyed, then guilt snagged at her chest; he was still missing.

She pushed aside the guilt and the growing anxiety about being victimized, and drew on her personal strength fueled by anger.

How arrogant of the killer to waltz into the command center and violate the team.

"I never should have left," Art McDonald said, shaking his head. "Eddie would still be here, he'd be okay."

"Don't be so hard on yourself, mate," Jeremy said. "Guilt is a worthless punishment when you have no control over the situation."

Good, maybe Max had gotten through to Jeremy after all.

Someone placed a hand to her shoulder. She wanted it to be Max's warm touch, but knew it wasn't.

"Are you okay?" Agent Kreegan asked.

"Yeah, I'm fine. How about you?"

"Better today. I remembered something and wanted to get with Eddie. I guess," She glanced around the room, "I was too late. If I'd only been five minutes earlier I might have—"

"Might have what, Agent Kreegan?" Max said, walking up to them. "Single-handedly taken on a serial killer? Stop beating yourself up. It's going to take a team of investigators to catch this bastard."

"Yes, sir," she said. "I was looking for Eddie because

I remembered something about the man who attacked me. A tattoo."

"Do we have a working computer?" Max called out.

"Over there, sir," Agent McDonald said.

"Art, are you comfortable enough with the computer to help Agent Kreegan find the image she's looking for?"

"Will do my best, guv."

Kreegan joined McDonald at his desk and they got to work.

"She looks traumatized," Cassie said.

"And you?"

She fidgeted under his scrutiny. No, she wouldn't let him be distracted because he was worried about her.

"I'm furious," she shot back, holding his gaze.

"Good, better furious than scared."

"Not much scares me anymore," she said. "I'll get started cleaning up so we don't feel like we're working in a war zone."

She started to walk away and he touched her arm.

"Thank you," he said.

"It's my job." She winked and got to work, picking up papers and folders from the floor.

When he thanked her, it sounded as if he thought this was the last place she wanted to be: in the midst of brutality and destruction.

Yet a part of her couldn't imagine being anywhere else. She couldn't imagine going a day without seeing Max. Placing a small notebook on Eddie's desk, she realized how much she wanted to be with Max, to help him solve murder cases and write his book. She wanted to share his life.

She'd been feeling this way for a while now, but only over the last few days had she really accepted the truth: she was falling for the edgy detective. She glanced at Max, who was in deep conversation with Jeremy. She'd been shocked and thrilled when he'd offered Jeremy absolution for his guilt over Max's injuries.

Something had definitely changed in Max. And she liked it.

"Is that Eddie's?"

Agent Kreegan's voice snapped Cassie from her daydream. She'd forgotten her hand was still resting on the small notebook. "I think so. I found it on the floor by his desk."

"Great, it might be able to help us." She snatched it from under Cassie's palm, and shoved it into her jacket pocket.

Cassie continued her clean-up efforts. As she picked up a folder, a gruesome photograph slipped to the floor. She shoved it back into the folder.

Truth was, she should be terrified that a killer had been so close. But she knew, deep in her heart, that Max would never let anything happen to her.

She knew that he cared about her. And the feeling was mutual.

"That's it!"

Cassie glanced up to see Agent Kreegan pointing at

the computer screen. Jeremy and Max rushed over to study the image.

"That's the tattoo on the guy's arm. He had me from behind, he…" She stood and backed away from the computer.

"It's all right," Max said, nodding to Jeremy.

With gentle encouragement, Jeremy led her away from the computer to sit down. For two guys who disliked each other, Max and Jeremy were great at nonverbal communication.

Cassie walked up beside him. The image on the computer screen looked like a skull with blood dripping out of its eyes.

"Where did you find this?" Max asked Agent McDonald.

"Agent Kreegan found a site for gang symbols. This one's for a drug cult called Apocalypse Red, an international group."

"A drug gang?" Max said.

Cassie sensed confusion in his voice.

"Sir, I found this upstairs taped to your window," Agent Spinelli said, coming into the room.

Cassie held her breath as Max slipped on gloves and unfolded a piece of paper.

His eyes flared. "Bloody hell. He's got Eddie. And we've got until eight tonight to find him."

Chapter Thirteen

"Let's focus on finding our man," Max said, his gut tangled in knots.

Lock it up, mate. It's the only way you'll save Eddie.

"I'll go up and dust for prints," Ruth said, grabbing her case and heading upstairs.

"I want everything on the drug cult," Max said. "Agent Barnes, call Bobby and have him find out if Lyle Cooper was into drugs. Something didn't ring true about his story and maybe this is it."

"What did the note say?" Jeremy asked.

Max handed it to him, not wanting to alarm the team by reading it aloud. Barnes's expression grew still. The bloke amazed him. He could be completely devastated and you'd never know it. Barnes's eyes snapped up to meet Max's, and Max knew he'd read the last line: *This one will die.*

And this case was a mess, Max thought, slipping off his gloves. A serial killer, but maybe not a serial killer, seemed out to get Max, yet Max had no connection with this vile drug gang.

"Check this out," Agent McDonald said. Max glanced at the computer. A man's image splashed across the screen: thirties, scraggly red hair and bloodshot eyes.

"This popped up off the FBI watch list of drug felons," McDonald said. "Rodney T. Barker, member of the Apocalypse Red gang, charged with murder, but it didn't stick. He's got a few other drug arrests, spent some time in jail. He's local."

"Spinelli, follow up on the drug gang," Max said. "I'll send Agent Kreegan downstairs to see if she can ID Mr. Barker."

The team split up, anxious to find Eddie. Max went up the stairs, hoping that if the bastard had been in his room long enough to tape a missive to his window, maybe he'd left a clue as well.

"Can I help?" Cassie said, catching up to him.

He glanced at her. "Help with what?"

"Whatever's put that look on your face. Whenever you're working through something, you get this blank stare in your eyes, almost like you've gone away."

"Really? Has anyone ever told you you've got natural detective skills?"

"Actually, yes."

"Who?"

"Jeremy," she said.

He must have made a face.

"You're jealous," she said.

"Of Jeremy Barnes? Nonsense."

They started down the hallway toward his room.

"Good, because you have nothing to be jealous about," she said.

"Why, because I'm a better investigator?"

"No, because I'm not attracted to Jeremy."

They paused outside his bedroom and she looked at him, challenging him to ask the next question: Was she attracted to Max?

They both knew the answer to that, and the feeling was mutual. But this wasn't the time for true confessions.

He stepped into the room. "Agent Kreegan, they need you to identify a suspect."

"I'm almost done here." She laid pressure-wound tape to the glass. "Since this is a rental, there's going to be tons of prints in the usual spots. I'm focusing on the glass where the tape left an impression. She peeled off the tape and pressed it to a lifting card. "If the killer's as smart as we think he is, I doubt he'll leave clues behind."

A few minutes passed, Max analyzing the contents of his room to determine if anything had been taken.

Kreegan packed up her supplies. "I'll get to work on the fingerprints and the note."

"Excellent."

She left and Max stood by the window, looking through the dusted glass.

"This drug connection doesn't feel right to you, does it?" Cassie asked.

"No," he said. "I'm having a hard time believing a drug dealer's gone mad and has decided to take up serial killing for a hobby."

"Maybe he was trying to throw us off the track with the serial killer angle."

He eyed her. "When did you get so smart?"

She blushed. "I didn't. Agent Kreegan suggested it."

He plucked a book from the floor, one of many that had been tossed from the shelf. "Setting up a crime scene to implicate someone takes a lot of thought. I'm not convinced a drug addict would have the brainpower to do that."

"Good point." Cassie's gaze drifted to the bed, then snapped up to meet Max's. She blushed.

Was that because of last night, or because of what she wished had happened last night?

Max slipped the book back onto the shelf and glanced out the window.

"Art was gone for only fifteen minutes. How is it possible that the killer knew precisely the moment to break in?"

Max pictured it in his mind, the killer walking up the stairs and knocking on the door, pretending to be with the utility company or phone company, and the second Eddie turned he clubbed him on the back of the head.

Eddie would lie there, helpless.

And it was Max's fault once again. Couldn't help him, couldn't help the innocent passengers at King's Cross. Four boys dead in London.

"Stop it!" Cassie grabbed his arm and shook him.

He blinked and glanced into her eyes.

"I can tell when you're going to that place," she said. "Knock it off. You'll never solve this case if you keep wallowing in all that guilt."

"Everything okay, guv?" Jeremy said from the door.

Bad, very bad. Max didn't want Jeremy knowing about his condition.

"I'm fine. Need some protein is all."

Jeremy glanced at Cassie, then back to Max. Once again, only God knew what the man was thinking.

"I've got Bobby on the mobile. I think you'd better speak with him."

Max straightened and reached for the phone, but Jeremy didn't release it right away. Concern filled the bloke's eyes.

"I'm fine," Max said, wrenching the phone from his second in command. "Bobby?"

"Hey, guv, I asked the Cooper boy about drugs. He had a complete breakdown, started sobbing, begging for forgiveness. It seems he and the Cunningham boy were dabbling in the recreational drug scene last month and that's why he blacked out. He wasn't sure what he'd taken, but it addled his brain to the point where he didn't know the difference between reality and fantasy. He thinks he may have had sex with a girl, and he's not sure it was consensual sex. It's ripping him apart. Seems like a nice kid, but the drugs made him crazy."

"Anyone else use the drugs?"

"He thinks a few of the boys at the fraternity."

"Find the fax number for the nurses' station. I'll have Jeremy fax over an image of a suspect. Show it to the boy."

"They gave him a sedative," Bobby said. "It will be a couple of hours before he regains consciousness."

"Bloody hell."

"There's something else," Bobby said. "I'm not sure it means anything, but the boy doesn't have a good luck coin, you know, like the one you found at the fraternity, the Goddess of Justice?"

Which meant it belonged to another fraternity member. Or it had been left by the killer.

"Keep watch for Jeremy's fax. You'll want to show it to Mr. Cooper the moment he wakes up."

"Yes, sir."

"Good work, Bobby."

"Thank you, sir."

Max flipped the phone closed and handed it to Jeremy.

"Bobby will phone you with the fax number of the nurses' station. Fax over a photograph of Rodney Barker for the Cooper boy to identify. We need a connection between our drug dealer and all three victims."

"Guv?" Jeremy questioned.

"My guess is the victim is injected with a drug to

make him powerless. That's why he willingly goes off with the killer. Remember the Cooper boy describing the alley? He heard a woman whimpering, and was stung by a bee. What if it was a hypodermic filled with a hallucinogen? The Cooper boy said he felt as though he was in a dream. Find me a connection, Jeremy."

"Yes, sir. Agent Kreegan isn't one hundred percent positive if it was Rodney Barker who attacked her. We're checking into a few other members of the Apocalypse Red gang."

"Very good. Cassie and I will join you in a minute."

Jeremy disappeared down the hallway.

"Do you want to talk about it?" Cassie said.

He glanced at her. "What?"

"Your attack?"

"No." He picked up his pack of cigarettes and placed them on the nightstand.

"What scares you?" Cassie asked.

"Besides you?" he joked.

"I'm serious."

"You want to know what scares me?" He plucked a ciggie from the pack and searched the room for a lighter. "Not finding the killer tops the list."

"But you're doing everything you can."

"Small comfort if we don't stop him." He gave up his search for a lighter and looked at her. "You don't know about the Edmonds boy."

"Who?"

"C.K.'s second victim in London—Charles Edmonds the third. By all accounts he was a nice, boring sort of chap. Worked hard in school, got excellent marks. He was an only child, and C.K. killed him. His father, Charles the second, blamed me for the boy's death."

"That's ridiculous."

"Just the same, the father nearly had my job. I was under an enormous amount of pressure to find the killer. Like I didn't put enough pressure on myself."

"What happened?"

He shot her a sarcastic grin. "I was blown up at King's Cross. Sometimes I wonder if I hadn't been under the threat of losing my job, if I hadn't been distracted by that pressure, I would have seen it coming."

"What?"

"The bombing. Maybe I would have noticed something out of place. Anyway, I tried returning to work, but between my physical condition and post-traumatic stress, I knew I would never return to SCI. I'd lost my edge."

"Seems to me like you've got it back."

"Maybe. My man is still out there being held against his will by a psychopath."

"Then let's stop wasting time up here brooding. Let's go find him." She took his hand and led him out of the room.

Out of his room, out of his misery and away from self-condemnation. They got to the top of the stairs and without thinking he turned and cupped her chin with his hand. "Thank you for so very many things."

It started as a gesture of thanks. Then, suddenly, she pulled him down to kiss her. A quick, yet passionate kiss. Good thing he had the cane to lean on.

She broke the kiss and smiled. "You're welcome. Let's find Eddie."

She went down the stairs ahead of him. That wasn't a friendly kiss, by any measure. It had been a while since he'd properly kissed a female, but he remembered what it was like to kiss a colleague…and what it felt like to kiss someone who meant much more.

Cassie had definitely worked her way into that second category. He started down the stairs and realized that after they'd solved this case, he should clarify their relationship, tell her that for her own good she should find herself a new job and forget about Max.

And if you can do that, you're a bloody miracle worker.

IT WAS after lunch and progress was slow. The Cooper boy hadn't regained consciousness since the morning's sedative, so Bobby couldn't have him look at pictures of suspects.

Spinelli was out chasing leads on the Apocalypse Red gang members, and Agents Kreegan and McDonald were out searching for evidence. Max noticed that Barnes, the master of self-control, was acting a little edgily.

Understandable, he thought, glancing at his watch.

One-thirty. They had only six and a half hours to find Eddie—hopefully, still alive.

Max had his doubts about that as well.

"Hey, guv," Art said, coming into the main room. "Agent Kreegan and I were searching the back alley and found these." He held up a syringe and a baseball cap.

"That's Eddie's hat," Cassie said.

Max glanced at the hat and remembered how the boy wore it to keep his wild hair under control. A nice bloke, Eddie, even if he talked too much.

"Check for prints. Determine what was in the syringe," he ordered.

"Yes, sir," Agent Kreegan said.

Max went to the kitchen and searched the fridge, shoving back images of Eddie being tortured and killed. The kid didn't deserve such a gruesome fate.

Unable to eat at a time like this, he closed the refrigerator door. Cassie stared up at him.

"How are you?" she said.

When he looked into her eyes he lost himself for a second, seeing only the goodness of life, hope and promise.

"I'm fine," he said.

But he wasn't fine. He had to appear strong for the rest of the team. Deep down his insides were being ripped apart.

Agent Spinelli swung open the back door. "I got nothin'. I mean *nothin'*. I checked out the last known address for Barker and it's an abandoned house on the south side. Sonofabitch," he muttered and stormed out of the kitchen, his heavy footsteps echoing down the hall.

With his arms spread across the counter, Max leaned forward and said, "I can't let him die."

"You can save him."

He eyed her. "If he's even still alive."

"What does your gut tell you?"

Someplace deep in his chest he felt hope. "I think he is." He glanced at her. "You said the post-traumatic stress disorder could have sharpened my sensitivity. I'm beginning to think you're right. But I'm also having a hard time making sense of things."

"Like what?"

"Elements of this case, for instance. Everything seems mixed up, out of order." He sighed. "I sound like an idiot."

"I've got an idea," she said. "Meet me upstairs."

He made his way to his room and lit a fag. With the first drag he became light-headed, sick to his stomach. Or was he sick from the thought of what was to come next? With a trembling hand he stabbed it out.

He was scared. Tough guy Max Templeton was scared because he hadn't a clue what Cassie planned to do to him. Was she going to make him relive his trauma to purge his system of the terror? No, he wasn't strong enough for that.

Bollocks. If reliving that hell would help them find Eddie, then so be it.

Someone knocked softly on his door.

"Come," he said, his nerves strung taught.

Cassie strode in carrying a large writing tablet, markers and a file. "Jeremy wanted you to see this—information about Rodney Barker."

Max scanned the details: Parents were deceased, but he had a stepfather in Chicago, and a sister in Detroit. Twenty-nine years old, Barker had been in and out of prison for the past ten years on various charges.

"We should get started," Cassie said, breaking his review of the Barker report.

"What are you going to do to me?"

"I'm going to help you organize your thoughts," she said with a smile. "What did you think I was going to do?"

"I wasn't sure."

"There's no time for that." She winked.

"I didn't mean—"

"I'm teasing. Come on. I'm a visual learner so I thought this might help you organize what's in your head."

She set up the writing tablet against the bookshelves and pulled out a marker. "Okay, we've got a killer, two dead boys, one kidnapped boy and one kidnapped agent." She drew circles and labeled them. "Then there's the four deaths in London."

"Wait, don't write that down. I don't think these are related to the London cases."

"Why?"

"Those murders stopped after our suspect died in a car accident. If by some chance that wasn't him in the car, why wait two years to start up again, and in a different country? Besides that, our London killer never got close to the investigative team. He was never that bold. No, this is a different killer."

"Good. What's next?"

"Connections between the victims. Write down— *college, fraternity* and *recreational drugs.*"

"A drug dealer attacked Agent Kreegan, there's another connection," she said.

She wrote the words *fraternity* and *drugs* under straight lines drawn from the victim's names.

"Now, tell me the things that have bothered you," she said. "Elements that have seemed odd about this case."

"The killer's proximity, always knowing our next move, leaving us love notes before actually taking a victim, the mysterious coin, Agent Kreegan being attacked outside the flat."

"Maybe she's close to finding the killer."

"We're not close, we're there." Max stood and went to Cassie's chart. "It's right in front of us. This bastard is always there, but he's always hiding behind someone, like a king hidden behind his front line in chess. The young man getting instructions in a phone booth. A woman calling the Cooper boy and luring him to the bar, then leaving him a note to meet out back. And right now—" he pointed to Rodney Barker's name "—I think he's our pawn. We get behind him, we find our killer."

Max grabbed his cane and started down the hall.

He felt Cassie behind him, always there to hold him up. He'd be lost without this girl.

He made his way down the stairs and into the front room.

"Guv," Art said, greeting him. "Agent Kreegan did some digging into old case files and found a record of working on one of Barker's drug busts."

Max looked at Kreegan, who seemed anxious. "I nailed the guy, but he got off on a technicality. What if this is about that case and has nothing to do with Eddie? God, I'd hate to be steering us in a wrong direction."

A wave of panic filled Max's chest.

Follow your instincts, mate.

"Barker is key," Max said. "And I think he has an accomplice."

"Why do you say that?" Kreegan asked.

"He's not smart enough to do this on his own—the kidnapping, staging, etcetera. We need to find him. Let's start with the stepfather."

"I've got an idea," Cassie said. "Who's got the step-father's phone number?"

Spinelli handed her a slip of paper. "The Chicago cops said Barker hasn't spoken with his stepfather in years. Besides, Henry Adler is an elder at his church, he'd have nothing to do with a criminal like Barker, even if he is his stepson."

She punched in the number. "Hello, Mr. Adler? This is the sweepstakes division of Universal Production companies and we're looking for a Rodney T. Barker. Yes, sir, he's won a prize. May I speak with him? Uh-huh. Thank you so much."

She hung up. "He doesn't live there, but he'll leave him a note on the garage, where he stores his personal items."

"Like kidnapped agents," Art said.

"I've got Adler's address on Harlem," Spinelli said.

"That's it. Everyone's going," Max ordered. "I'm not letting any of you out of my sight until we've nailed this bastard. Agent Barnes, we'll need equipment."

"It's covered."

Max looked at Cassie, placing a hand to her shoulder. "You understand why I won't leave you here?"

"Yes."

For a split second he felt a connection to her that eased his anxiety.

"I've got directions," Spinelli said, grabbing a sheet of paper from the printer.

"Let's get to it, then," Max said.

They filed out to the SUV, Max focused on finding Eddie, safe and alive.

Adrenaline started to hum low in his gut. He sensed the rest of his team strung taut with nerves. Jeremy's white-knuckled fingers on the steering wheel belied his controlled appearance.

The car was dead silent except for Spinelli's verbal directions. Twenty minutes later Spinelli motioned for Barnes to pull to the curb.

"The stepfather's house is the red brick number across the street," Spinelli explained. "The garage is out back, in the alley."

"We should make contact with the stepfather so he doesn't call police when he sees us on his property," Max said.

Barnes turned to address the team. "Everyone wears a vest. I've got them in the back, along with firearms."

Max glanced into the back seat. "Barnes and Spinelli, check out the garage while McDonald and I make introductions to the stepfather. Agent Kreegan and Cassie, stay in the car."

"I'd rather come, sir," Agent Kreegan said. "In case you need medical aid for Eddie."

"Fine. Cassie, keep the doors locked."

He got out and went around back where Jeremy handed out vests and firearms. He handed Max a gun that looked familiar.

"Left this behind in London," Jeremy said.

"Thanks." Max secured his weapon, appreciating Barnes even more. "McDonald and I will meet you, Spinelli and Kreegan out back."

"Yes, sir," Jeremy said.

The three agents disappeared around the corner.

Max took position next to the door. Art McDonald pressed the doorbell. Once. Twice.

Someone pulled back the window covering and Art

placed his Scotland Yard ID to the glass. The front door opened.

"Yes?" an older man said.

"Mr. Adler?"

"Yes."

"We're looking for Rodney T. Barker."

"He doesn't live here."

"I understand, sir. We're running a private investigation and would like your permission to—"

A gunshot echoed from the back of the house.

"Go inside and lock the doors," Max ordered the stepfather.

McDonald raced around back.

Max ripped his firearm from the holster and, leaning heavily on his cane, hobble-skipped to the back of the house. Art grabbed him by the vest and pulled him to the ground, next to a cement planter. "Get down, guv."

Max studied the garage, tall and white, with a broken window up top.

"I think Barnes and his team are inside," Art said.

The side door to the garage burst open and a man jumped out, waving a gun and yelling. "The angel of death will find you! Take you to the park and slay you. Red blood dripping from your eyes, she'll love you until you die."

"Mr. Barker, we'd like to talk to you," Max called. "Could you put down your weapon?"

"Dance and dance, and spin and bleed, and drink

and dance and spin again." He twirled in circles like a child pretending to be a ballerina.

"Stoned," Max said.

"Bloody looped," Art agreed.

"A gun, for fun, drink rum, go numb!" He tossed the gun to the ground and a shot rang out.

At first Max thought the thrown gun had discharged, then he spotted Agent Kreegan standing by the garage, her gun drawn.

She'd shot him.

Max and Art jumped from their hiding spot and raced across the alley. McDonald kicked the gun away from the suspect and knelt down to feel for a pulse. He nodded to Max that the man was dead. Kreegan still stood there, gun drawn.

"It's done now," McDonald said to her, pushing on her arms to lower her weapon.

Max went into the darkened garage and tripped on something. He caught his balance and looked down.

And there, on the hard cement lay Jeremy Barnes.

Chapter Fourteen

Max fell to his knees beside Jeremy. This was unacceptable. Jeremy was not dead. Max wouldn't allow it.

Keep your wits, old boy. He's wearing a vest.

Someone slid open the door, lighting the garage. "Guv?" Art said.

"Eddie's up here!" Spinelli called from the loft. "He's alive. I'll bring him down."

Max felt for Jeremy's pulse. Slow and steady.

"I've never seen him like this." Art knelt beside Jeremy's still form. "He looks so beaten."

"He'll be fine." Max spotted a bullet lodged in the vest. Barnes was going to be sore. Max hoped there weren't any serious internal injuries.

"Jeremy? Wake up, mate," Max encouraged.

Jeremy moaned and rolled onto his side, hugging his midsection. "Since when was I ever your mate?" he muttered.

A breath of relief escaped Max's lips.

"Brilliant, guv," Art said. "He's okay."

"I'm not okay, I'm bloody furious," Jeremy said. He tipped his head back and eyed Max. "You look like hell. Didn't you catch the bastard?"

"Agent Kreegan shot him," Max said, then nodded to Art to check on Kreegan.

"Good," Jeremy said. "Eddie, he's up in the loft."

"We know. What happened?"

"Spinelli got in through a window up top. I told Kreegan to watch the back of the garage, and I tried sneaking in the front." He coughed and winced in pain. "Bad move on my part."

"Wouldn't be your first," Max joked.

Jeremy glared. "Help me up."

"You sure you don't want to relax for a second?"

"Ah, don't coddle me, Templeton."

Max propped Jeremy up with an arm around his shoulder.

"Ambulance is on its way," McDonald said, from the doorway. "Agent Kreegan is pretty messed up."

"Why's that?" Barnes asked.

"The suspect had dropped his firearm before she shot him," McDonald explained.

Barnes looked at Max. "She did the right thing. Case closed."

Max wasn't so sure.

THE GROUP was in rare form, laughing and toasting their way into the evening. The Blackwell team had been given two weeks and had solved the case in less than four days. Not bad for a first project, Jeremy thought, packing up files on his desk.

Once the Chicago cops finished with the crime scene, it was pretty obvious that Barker was their killer from the start. Personal effects from the two victims were found in the garage loft, along with a Mardi Gras-type mask and vials of a mysterious drug being tested by police. They even found a laptop, and upon analyzing its Internet history, found all kinds of searches about the Crimson Killer case.

A drug connection between the victims and Barker was under investigation. The preliminary theory was that the college boys had been selling Barker's drugs to schoolmates, but wanted to stop. Barker said they couldn't and they threatened to go to the police, forcing his hand.

Still, Max didn't seem happy. He couldn't understand why two boys, with no criminal background, had suddenly become drug dealers. He questioned Lyle Cooper's connection, since the boy refused to admit he'd ever sold drugs.

Of course he wouldn't admit it. He'd go from a hospital room to a prison cell.

Jeremy studied Max as he leaned back in an office chair observing, not participating in the celebration. Then Cassie knelt beside him and whispered something into his ear.

Maybe his concern had less to do with solving this

case and more to do with his cute blond assistant. He'd be a fool to turn away from that sweet girl. But knowing Max, he'd ruin it for himself. At least that's what he usually did. Almost as though he was punishing himself.

For what? They'd found Eddie in time. The agent was recuperating in the hospital. All was well.

His mobile went off. Jeremy ambled into the kitchen where it was quiet.

"Barnes," he said.

"I got your voice mail. Congratulations," the Patron said.

"Thank you, sir."

"I'm in New York on business. I plan to fly into Chicago tomorrow morning to meet the team and congratulate them."

"I thought you said you wanted to be anonymous."

"I've changed my mind. I'd like to make you and Templeton an offer. I need to do that in person. Expect me around ten."

"Yes, sir."

"And Barnes, don't reveal my identity quite yet."

"If you think that's best."

"I do."

The line went dead.

Jeremy went into the front room and turned off the music. Everyone looked up. "The Patron of Blackwell wants to meet with us tomorrow, mid-morning, to congratulate everyone in person."

"Is he going to give us a bonus for finding the killer so quickly?" Bobby asked.

"A bonus? You? All you did was sit at the hospital and flirt with the nurses," Art teased.

"Hey, I tell you what, why don't I call a couple of them to meet up with us at a pub?"

Bobby whipped out his mobile.

"How about it, guv?" Art asked Max. "You up for a little pub crawling?"

"Not tonight. But you go, have a good time."

"You sure?" Art said.

"Yes, and that's an order." Max started toward the steps.

"Count me in," Jeremy said, hoping to corral the lot of them out of the house to give Max and Cassie privacy.

"Brilliant!" Bobby said, snapping his flip phone closed. "Nurse Monroe is coming and she's bringing her roommate."

"I'm too old for this," Art said.

"Yeah, old man McDonald," Finn taunted.

Spinelli followed them to the door.

"You coming, love?" Bobby asked Cassie.

"No, I'm really tired. But thanks."

"I'll be right out," Jeremy said, then pulled Cassie aside. "You all right?"

"Sure." She rubbed her arms as if chilled. "Just worried about you-know-who."

"What's Templeton done now?"

"He's not sure you got the right man."

"He's not used to solving a case so quickly. He'll warm up to the idea. Cheers."

She smiled. "Have fun."

"What, babysitting this gang of misfits?"

"What's going on?" Agent Kreegan asked, coming out of the kitchen.

"We're going out. Want to join us?" Jeremy offered.

"No. I have to get home for my daughter. She's had a rough couple of months. Teenagers," she sighed.

A car honked outside. "Can we give you a lift?" Jeremy asked Agent Kreegan.

"No. I've got my car."

"Very well, then. Good night, ladies."

He joined the group out front.

"You're not going with them?" Agent Kreegan asked.

"No, I'm going to hang back." Cassie's gaze drifted up the stairs.

Agent Kreegan smiled. "I don't blame you. Well, good night."

Kreegan went out the front door and Cassie locked it behind her. She welcomed the quiet, the peace.

"Cassie?" Max said from the top of the stairs.

Her heart jumped. "Yes?"

"May I have a word with you?"

She swallowed back a ball of nerves and started up

the stairs. She'd read the attraction in his eyes a moment ago. She cared so much for this man.

She went to his room. He wasn't there. "Max?"

He opened the bathroom door, wearing only a towel around his waist. "It's an old house, but they've got a Jacuzzi tub. I could use a soak, my hip…"

"Oh, right."

"Come here." He smiled, grabbed her wrist and pulled her against his naked chest. "I thought we'd start with a bath and work our way to the bed."

She didn't respond at first. He looked into her eyes. "Only if you want to."

"I want to," she said, "very much."

He led her into the bathroom, where a candle cast a fiery glow on the tiled walls and water filled the tub. She started to unbutton her pants, but he placed his hand to hers. "Let me do it."

With great precision he peeled off each layer of clothing until she stood in her bra and underpants. Holding her against him, he unhooked her bra, his gentle hands slipping between the lace and her skin. He slid it completely off and cupped her breasts with such reverence that her legs started to wobble.

"I've wanted you for a very long time," he whispered into her hair, then skimmed his hands around her back, to her buttocks.

He slid one hand between her skin and her underwear. His other hand cupped her chin, tipping her face so she could look into his eyes.

"I'm absolutely mad about you," he whispered.

He kissed her, the warmth of his lips spreading across her body to her fingertips. She'd never felt this kind of tenderness, this kind of heat. For a brief second it scared her. Then she remembered this was Max, a man with more integrity than anyone she'd ever met. A man who had come so far in accepting his physical condition and emotional trauma these past few days.

Earlier he'd thanked her for challenging him out of his self-imposed darkness, and said he wanted to make tonight special.

So far he was doing a bang-up job.

He deepened the kiss and she found herself wishing that they were in a soft bed, instead of standing on cold tile. Her nipples peaked against his lightly haired chest, aching for something she couldn't name.

He broke the kiss. "I don't have the patience for the bath," he said, breathing heavily against her lips.

"Thank God," she joked.

He studied her expression and kissed her again, only this time, he picked her up.

"Your hip," she protested.

"I'm fine."

With Cassie in his arms, he leaned over the tub. "Hit the water, will you?"

She twisted the knob and water stopped running.

"Good girl," he whispered. In a jerky motion, he carried her into her bedroom.

She knew it had to be hurting him, but she also knew he wanted to prove something to her.

He placed her on the comforter. A streetlight reflected through her window, casting a soft glow across the room.

"Let me see you," he said, running a hand between her breasts and down, past her belly button. She arched to make the connection, and when his fingers grazed her soft curls, she felt a moan rise from deep in her chest.

"You are a beautiful and amazing woman," he whispered, shifting onto the bed beside her.

"Make love to me," she demanded.

Slowly, tenderly, he shifted her on top so she could take the lead. He cradled her breasts, stroking her nipples in such a way that she thought she'd completely lose it. She realized he wanted her to. He wanted her to let go, give in to the attraction that had been growing between them for the past few months.

With her hands to his chest, she straddled him, opening to his need, absorbing his power. He reached between them and stroked her. She was going to come apart in his arms.

"Let go," he whispered.

He stroked, thrust his hips, and stroked again. She cried out as she flew across the heavens. She heard him groan, then go still, guiding her to his chest. His heart beat strong and steady, just like the man.

And she knew, for once in her life, that this was love.

Chapter Fifteen

The next morning Max showered, got dressed and packed his things. He was anxious to get back to Seattle and his life with Cassie.

His life with Cassie. God, he was lucky as hell.

He went to Cassie's room to give her the open plane ticket. He figured she'd want to stay a day or two to visit her mother. He wouldn't assume she'd want his company for that, but he'd stay if asked.

He started to knock on her door but thought better of it. *Let the poor girl sleep.* He'd worn her out last night. They'd worn each other out, making love, talking, holding one another until three in the morning.

Then they'd fallen asleep in each other's arms, until a nightmare woke him. He didn't want to keep Cassie up, so he went into his own room to give her peace.

He slipped the ticket under her door and headed downstairs. Some of the team had assembled in the front room, snacking on pastries and drinking coffee. Max went into the kitchen.

"Have a good time last night?" Max asked Jeremy.

"Not as good as you," he teased.

"Hey, has anyone seen Cassie?" Eddie asked, coming into the kitchen.

"You should be in the hospital," Max scolded.

"I'm fine. Checked myself out this morning. Wouldn't miss this meeting. Where's Cassie?"

"Still asleep," Max said, pouring himself a cup of coffee.

"Did she go clubbing with you guys?"

"No, actually." Jeremy glanced at Max. "She didn't."

The doorbell rang. "I'll get it," Jeremy said.

Max went to the front room, accepting congratulations and good wishes. He'd come around to believing they'd caught the killer. After all, the evidence supported as much. Who was he to argue with it?

"I'd like to introduce the Patron of Blackwell," Jeremy said. "Charles Edmonds."

Max snapped his attention to the doorway. Bloody hell.

"Mr. Edmonds is here to congratulate you and offer you a permanent spot on the team," Jeremy continued, his gaze intent on Max.

Max put down his mug, strode past Edmonds without saying a word, and went out the front door.

"Templeton!" Jeremy called.

Max slammed the door and started for the sidewalk.

"Where are you going?" Jeremy demanded from the landing.

"Any place but here."

Jeremy caught up to him on the sidewalk. "Charles Edmonds founded the Blackwell Group, so what? His motivation is honorable and he's got plenty of money to keep this thing going."

"He made my life hell back in London. Have you forgotten?"

"That was over a year ago. Move on, for God's sake. At least listen to the man. Then make your decision."

"You lied to me, you bastard."

"I didn't tell you it was Charles because I knew your pride would get the better of you and you wouldn't join the team. I needed you to help find a killer. Can't you shelve your pride for once?"

He marched up the stairs and disappeared into the house. Max stood there, dumbfounded. Then the front door opened and Charles Edmonds stepped out.

He took a deep breath and glanced at Max. "How's the hip?"

"You're kidding, right?"

"I'm trying to be polite."

"Good luck."

He sighed. "Templeton, I know I've wronged you in the past and I'm sorry. Losing Charlie was the single worst thing that's ever happened to me." He paused and glanced at the sky. "I've struggled ever since to make sense of it." He pinned Max with his steely gray eyes. "I've created Blackwell to keep Charlie's memory alive. This team," He motioned toward the house, "exists for the sole purpose of solving crimes, maybe even saving other parents the devastating grief that Melinda and I had to endure. It's my mission to see it thrive. I hope you decide to stay on and help Jeremy."

"Pardon me if I struggle to process this, Charles. You nearly had me lynched in London."

"I'm trying to make up for that. I lost my mind for a while. The only way I got it back was by creating this group. Blackwell was the name of Charlie's horse…" His voice drifted off.

Max's resolve started to crack. The man had lost his son, after all.

"I don't like being manipulated," Max said.

"I know. And I'm sorry. Jeremy didn't think you'd help, what between the hatred you felt for me and the resentment towards him. I wish you'd consider leading the team. Well, I've said my piece." He turned and went back into the house.

Max stood for a good five minutes trying to process this latest development. He remembered the brutal things Edmonds had accused him of: being a liar and a volatile and incompetent investigator. He'd even attacked Max's scruples, that one.

Because he was in pain, because he'd lost a beloved son, a boy he loved with all his heart.

Still, Jeremy should have told Max who was footing the bill.

And Max would have never made this trip and found a killer. He wouldn't have fallen in love.

He eyed the second floor where Cassie slept. He'd never felt this way before, safe and loved. The way she'd opened herself to him with such unconditional acceptance had awakened a part of his soul he hadn't known existed. That couldn't have been easy for her, not with her history.

His mobile vibrated, indicating he'd received a text message.

He retrieved the message:

She will die unless you come. Alone. Ba'hai Temple. Noon.

The number was blocked. Chills shot across his shoulders.

"Cassie," he whispered, climbing the stairs into the house. He pushed though the front door and tore upstairs.

"What is it?" Jeremy called after him.

Max ignored him, reaching Cassie's door and knocking, softly.

"Cassie, are you there, love?"

He knew in his gut she wasn't. Not after that text message. He flung open her door and studied the room, all her belongings, her picture frame, robe, suitcase, still in place.

Max had been right: Barker had an accomplice, most likely the real killer.

The real killer had Cassie.

"Max?" Jeremy said, joining him in Cassie's room. "What's happened?"

"She's gone," was all he dared say. She was gone and if he didn't meet a killer at noon, alone, she'd be dead.

"Maybe she's gone out for a bite," Jeremy said. "She'll be back. Her things are still here."

Get it together. Alone *meant without the team.*

Reality struck him hard in the chest—the killer had a connection to the team, that's why he always knew their next move, where Max was at any given moment, and how to break into the command center. Max couldn't trust any of them.

"Max?" Jeremy said. "Come downstairs and listen to what Charles has to offer."

Snap to it, old boy. Get your wits back and pretend you aren't on the brink of losing the love of your life.

Blast, if he had only stayed with her, held her all night long, the killer couldn't have gotten to her.

But how? Did the killer snatch her from her bed? And no one had heard anything? Impossible.

His mind spun as he followed Jeremy downstairs into the meeting. With one part of his brain he listened to the proposal for the continuation of Blackwell, and with the other side he mapped out his next move.

"Please consider my proposal," Edmonds said to the

group. "I'd like to keep the team up and running inde-
finitely. I can offer a modest salary, all expenses paid,
plus a retirement program."

"Hear that, Art? Retirement." Bobby slugged Art
in the arm.

"Very funny," Art shot back.

"Jeremy Barnes is your contact person," Edmonds said.

"You staying on, guv?" Bobby asked.

Max glanced at him, unable to process his question.
"I'm not sure, Bobby. I've got some things to work out."

"He's a big-time author now, going to make the best-
seller list with your first book, aren't ya', guv?" Art added.

Max forced a smile.

"That's it, then," Jeremy dismissed the team. "Enjoy
the day. Take in the sites, ride to the top of the John
Hancock. Be a tourist and we'll meet back at five to
make final plans."

The group split up and Max sought out Agent Spinelli.
"Have you heard of this place, the Ba'hai Temple?"

"Yeah, it's up on the north shore," Spinelli said.

"Does the tube take you up there?"

"You mean the train? Yeah. Drops you off at Linden
about two blocks from the temple."

"Excellent, thanks."

Max turned and nearly bumped into Jeremy.

"Taking in the sights?" Jeremy said, disbelief in his
voice.

"What of it?"

"Mind if I join you?"

"I'd mind very much." He brushed past Jeremy and went outside to compose himself.

Hold it together. She's depending on you.

IF HE WEREN'T looking for a killer Max would be having a grand time strolling the gardens surrounding the temple. As each minute passed, he grew more and more anxious. There was no sign of Cassie, no sign of anything out of the ordinary.

His mobile beeped with a text message.

Inside. Movie room.

He snapped the phone closed and headed to the lower level. As he approached the film room, something caught his eye on the floor: a gold locket.

Cassie's necklace. He bent down to pick it up and a wave of dizziness filled his head.

"God, no," he said, fear stabbing his shoulders.

He tried to focus, but his mind spun with panic. He'd done this, put her in the path of a killer. He'd subjected her to the brutalities of a murderer's games, and now, the love of his life would die. He was having another attack, brought on by grief.

No, it didn't mean she was dead. It meant the killer wasn't done with him.

"Sir? Are you all right?"

Someone spoke to him, but he couldn't get his bearings. Still off, losing balance. Opening his fist, he studied the locket in his palm.

Fairy dust, to fly away.

"Agent Templeton?".

Max glanced up at Agent Kreegan standing beside him, a concerned expression on her face.

"What are you doing here?" he said.

"Agent Barnes sent me. He was worried so we followed you."

"That bastard." He struggled to breathe against the assault of his panic attack. "We'll never find her now." He pushed away from the wall, but wavered.

"Take it easy, sir. Let me help." She grabbed his arm and steadied him.

They walked outside into the sunshine, but he felt no warmth. Cassie would die because of him.

"Where is…he?" Max asked, struggling to form words. This was the worst episode to be sure. And he felt himself succumbing to it, giving up.

Cassie was gone.

"No," he said, his voice weak.

"Agent Barnes is waiting in the car," Kreegan said.

"That sonofabitch. I swear…I'll kill him."

A few more steps, floating, drifting, Cassie was gone. His heart was being ripped from his chest. He loved her, had to tell her now. But there was no now, only blackness.

Death.

He'd failed again, only this time, Cassie would be the one to die.

Chapter Sixteen

"My daughter barely speaks."

Max heard the woman's voice, but couldn't open his eyes: so tired, as if he'd taken too much Vicodin. He'd been tempted once, tempted to swallow a dozen instead of one.

To go to sleep and never wake up.

But that was before Cassie had come into his life.

He struggled to focus. Where was he?

"She'll never be the same."

That voice, familiar, but not Cassie's.

Cassie. He'd gone to save her. Went to…the temple and found…her locket.

"Cassie?" It came out in a whisper. An ache. He'd die if anything had happened to her.

"You wouldn't leave it alone, even though you had the perfect suspect."

He opened his eyes, but couldn't quite focus.

"Cassie?"

"She's gone."

"No!" he howled. He pulled on his wrists. They were pinned in place. "Cassie!" Adrenaline shot his vision into focus.

Ruth Kreegan, the Blackwell forensics expert stood over him.

"Agent Kreegan?" he said, confused as hell.

"Those boys? They sexually assaulted my daughter," she said. "There was no remorse, no regret."

He was sitting in a car, his wrists bound to the steering wheel.

"Themis, the Goddess of Justice," she said. "That's me. I had to do it. We both know how flawed the judicial system is."

"No," is all he could say. He was so weak, so confused. She'd drugged him, probably with the same substance she'd used on the murder victims.

"Cheryl couldn't defend herself so I had to do it for her. Those arrogant, spoiled college boys destroyed my baby girl."

"Ruth," he croaked.

"I thought you'd want this." She placed something in his hand.

Cassie's locket.

His chest tightened with grief.

"No!" He opened his hand and the locket bounced off the seat and hit the floor.

Breathe, come on, mate. But his lungs had tightened

to near paralysis. He struggled against the effect of the drug she'd given him.

"What did you do?" he demanded.

"What was necessary."

But she hadn't murdered Cassie. He simply couldn't accept it.

"Why?" he said, hoping to buy time, struggling to think.

"Justice," Ruth said. "Honor."

"Where's the honor…in killing an innocent woman?"

"Where's the honor in what they did to my baby girl?" she cried, her voice shrill. "But I made it right," she said, her voice more controlled. "I maneuvered my way onto your team and kept you off track. I even set up that bastard Barker as the murderer. I've wanted to get rid of him ever since he paid me off to falsify lab results. I needed the money for my only daughter, my princess. It's just the two of us since my husband left. She's my whole world."

She stroked his forehead and he jerked away.

"I knew you'd never stop, and I'm not done," Ruth said. "I have to kill the Cooper boy. I'd almost finished, but you went to the bar where I'd snatched him. You're good, Templeton. Too good."

She stroked his cheek and he thought he'd be sick. "Don't." He yanked on his bindings.

He felt her reach across him and turn on the car.

"No!" a woman shrieked.

Kreegan was pulled out of the car. Max struggled to clear his head. It was no use.

Someone jumped into the car beside him. "Drive!" Cassie ordered.

"Cassie?" His heart ached. He wanted to tell her he loved her, wanted to make sure she knew.

"Drive!"

"Drugged, blurred vision," he croaked.

She shifted next to him and grabbed the steering wheel. "Hit the accelerator."

He pressed his right foot to the accelerator and they jerked backward.

"Brake!" she cried.

He hit the brake, shoving Cassie against the dash. He heard her shift gears.

"Go!"

He pressed the pedal again and they took off, across rugged soil. A sharp turn shoved her into his chest, then she spun the wheel and they straightened.

Shots rang out behind them.

"Faster," she ordered.

He shoved his foot to the floor, picking up speed.

"Jeremy!" she cried.

She jerked the wheel and they spun in a circle.

"Brake!"

They knocked up against something. Everything went still.

He couldn't feel her against his chest anymore.

"Cassie?"

A hissing sound answered him. He opened his eyes;

saw the blurred images of people running toward him. He thought he saw Cassie slumped against the passenger door.

He was desperate to reach out. Couldn't move. His wrists still bound to the steering wheel. He struggled to stay conscious. Make sense of it all.

Agent Kreegan was the killer?

Men's voices mumbled outside the car.

"Cassie?" he said.

"It's okay, guv," Bobby said. "They're taking her to the hospital."

Max had to get to her. Had to tell her.

More voices. *Explosive device…timer…steering wheel.*

"Max, it's Jeremy. Cassie is fine. We've got to get you out of this car, but it's a tricky proposition. Can you hear me? Can you do what I tell you?"

"Never."

"No joking, guv." Jeremy's voice sounded deeper than usual. "Kreegan's ex-husband was an explosives expert and we think she's rigged the car. You have to focus and do exactly what I tell you."

"Guv?" Bobby said from the door. "We've got five, maybe ten seconds so I'm going to pull you out and then run like the wind."

Bloody hell, they were all going to die.

"Jeremy, don't—"

"Listen to Bobby," Jeremy said. "On three he's going to pull you to safety. One, two…three."

Max felt something tug at his wrists, freeing them.

Bobby pulled him from the car, put Max over his shoulder and ran. Sirens wailed, piercing his eardrums. Bobby grunting. Running. Holding on to Max.

An explosion rocked the ground and they fell against the hard earth.

Chapter Seventeen

Cassie awakened and struggled to get her bearings.

Oh God, Max. He'd been in the car, and they'd been speeding away from that crazy woman who kidnapped her and shot at them as they made their escape. Then she'd seen Jeremy and the team, and she'd spun the wheel, hit a tree and—

"Max!" Her eyes shot open and she sat up.

"Shh."

She snapped her gaze to the man sitting beside her on her bed. Max.

"You're okay." She reached for him and he wrapped his arms around her. She held on, rocking a little, feeling his strength and inhaling his scent. She wanted this man in her life until the very end.

"Relax," he said. "You need your rest."

Something in his voice bothered her. She leaned against the pillow and studied him. He looked unusually controlled today, almost too much so.

"I'd like a few details, if you're up to it," he said in a businesslike tone.

"Sure."

"How did you end up with Agent Kreegan?"

"She woke me at five. Said you were having trouble and needed me, that she couldn't do it alone. I was pretty sleepy, from the night before." She glanced at him and blushed. "I automatically went with her. I thought maybe you were having a spell and needed me."

His grip tightened on the brass handle of his cane. "Yet you managed to get away from her?"

"All that self-defense training finally paid off." She smiled.

He didn't.

"So, she was the killer all along?" she said.

"Yes. Apparently the boys sexually assaulted her daughter. The girl has not recovered."

"Wow." Cassie studied him, but he wouldn't make eye contact. "How are you feeling?" This case couldn't have eased his post-trauma anxiety.

He jumped to his feet, pacing to the foot of the bed. "How am I feeling? she asks." He stared her down. "Did you know the car was set to explode?"

"Yes, before I got away, Agent Kreegan told me her plan to kill you, us, by sending the car into the ravine and blowing it up to destroy as much evidence as possible."

"Yet you climbed in beside me."

"Of course. I…" She hesitated, not sure if she should say it. "I love you."

He squeezed the handle of his cane and leaned into it slightly. "You put yourself in grave danger because of me. I can't have that."

She sensed where this was going. Tough, she wasn't going to let him get away with it.

"I'm a big girl, Max. I make my own decisions."

"And they land you in the hospital. You've got stitches across your forehead, and cracked ribs. You were nearly killed, for God's sake. Because of me."

"I'm fine. It isn't nearly as bad as what Karl did to me."

The moment the words escaped her lips, she realized her mistake. She'd compared her injuries from saving Max to her abusive husband's beatings.

She closed her eyes. That's not what she'd meant. She'd meant that she was tough, damn it. She'd defended herself against her kidnapper. She'd used self-defense skills to get away from Agent Kreegan, then she'd slid down the ravine and waited. She knew Kreegan planned to kidnap Max, and Cassie had to help him.

Cassie, a formerly abused wife, was now a tough woman who could defend herself against a murderer. That's why Cassie was perfect for Max—she was strong, and Max needed a strong woman who could deal with his line of work, and help him work through his post-traumatic stress.

"That didn't come out right." She opened her eyes.

He stood by the window, looking outside. "I won't leave Chicago until you're ready. But you need to know, this thing that's started between us," He turned to her, "it has no future."

She wanted to slap him, jump from her bed and whack him over the head with his cane. "Why not?"

"I can't bear the thought of putting you in danger," he said. "You deserve better."

She deserved Max. That's what she knew, deep in her heart.

She also knew that every second he looked at her bruised and scratched up face he blamed himself. And that tore him apart.

Because he loved her.

She couldn't force him to accept that, any more than she could force him to see how perfect they were together. As he stood there, that tortured look in his pale-green eyes, her chest ached. It broke her heart to think he was going to walk out of her room and out of her life.

Because he cared so much about her.

"How's Jeremy?" she said, making small talk.

"He's recovering. Bloody fool nearly got blown up."

His gaze drifted to the floor, as if he were uncomfortable.

She closed her eyes, exhaustion taking hold. Emotional exhaustion.

"Right, well, I'll head up to see Jeremy." He walked

to her bedside. "I'm so sorry." He leaned forward and kissed her, a soft, tender kiss.

She relished the feel of his mouth on hers, and she was determined to feel this again. He broke the kiss, their lips still inches apart.

"Take care," he said.

I love you, she heard.

He left the room and she wrapped her arms around her midsection. "You're not getting away that easily," she whispered. But today she was too tired to fight.

"I SHOULD bloody kill you for pulling that stunt."

Even without his glasses, Jeremy knew the voice belonged to Max.

"It's my job." He reached for his glasses, his shoulder aching in protest. The blast had thrown him against an unforgiving tree.

"Here." Max handed him the rimless specs.

Jeremy placed them on the bridge of his nose and studied his boss. "You're here to torture me, then?"

Max stared at Jeremy with anger in his eyes—and something else. Something like concern? It must have been Max standing at his bedside in the middle of the night. Jeremy had awakened with a start to a man standing over him. But when he'd asked who was there, the form had dissolved into the shadows.

Max probably didn't want Jeremy to know how much he cared.

"I should fire you," Max said.

Jeremy smiled. "We're not at Scotland Yard anymore, remember?"

"Of course I remember. My brain's not completely addled from that drug."

"So," Jeremy narrowed his eyes. "You'll lead Blackwell?"

"Not if you can't learn to take orders." He leaned back in his chair, resting his hands on the top of his cane. It suited him today, looked like he'd grown into it.

"How did you find us?" Max said.

"I thought about what you said, about Barker not being our murderer. I grilled Eddie about the abduction and he remembered some odd things like chasing purple turtles on his grandparents' farm, stealing cupcakes from the corner store, and Agent Kreegan smashing his computer. He thought it was an effect of the drug. It bothered me how the killer was one step ahead of us. I dug into Kreegan's background and discovered that her daughter's name is Cheryl, the same name as the girl the Cooper boy had the affair with. Made some calls, found out Cheryl hadn't been to school this term. A friend told us she'd been attacked by some college boys and hadn't recovered. We pieced it together."

"You had a busy afternoon."

"Eddie checked phone records. She and Barker were in contact. It all fell into place. I called her cell phone and kept her on the line with questions about the case. Eddie traced the call to an area in Winnetka. We were driving around when we heard gunshots. We found you, pulled Cassie from the car and took Agent Kreegan into custody. Cassie said something about a bomb."

"Aren't you the smart one?" Max said.

Jeremy eyed him. A compliment? "Thanks."

"Book-smart, not street-smart."

"I'm sorry?"

"You jumped into a car you knew was set to explode." He stood, pacing to the foot of the bed. "You should have waited for a bomb unit."

"We had to get you out of there."

"So you climbed inside and ordered Bobby to help you?"

"I didn't order Bobby. He insisted."

"And you all think *I'm* mad."

Jeremy smiled.

Max sighed. "I'm still stunned about Agent Kreegan, a killer, right beside us all along, throwing us off track, knowing our next move. She was a chemist, did you know that?"

"No."

"Police think she developed the hallucinogenetic drug used on the victims. I also suggested to local police that Kreegan caused our original forensics expert's car accident."

"All that for revenge?"

"Grief and anger will drive people to do crazy things. We also suspect her injuries from the false attack were caused when the Cooper boy escaped. He knocked her about pretty good. Oh, and police found the victims' drivers' licenses at her house."

"Kept as trophies?" Jeremy asked.

"Apparently. And she set up Barker as the murderer."

"And killed him. How convenient."

"Quite."

"How's your girl?" Jeremy said.

Max held his gaze. "Cassie is recovering."

"I want an invitation to the wedding. I've earned it."

"I wish I could accommodate you."

Jeremy struggled to sit up. "You'd better put me on the bloody guest list."

"I can't," Max hesitated. "I won't allow her to marry into this violence. I care too much for her."

"You're running away from the best thing that's happened to you."

"Did they make you a psychiatrist while you've been in here?"

"That girl wants nothing more than to take care of you for the rest of her life," Jeremy said. "She's crazy about you and you're pushing her away?"

Max stood and paced to the window and back. "You didn't see her. She's black and blue, she's got stitches." He motioned to his forehead. "I won't put her through that again. She's too fragile."

"Are we talking about the same woman? The woman who saved you from a serial killer?"

"Aren't you listening? I won't be responsible for her getting hurt."

"Bloody hell, Templeton, stop being responsible for the entire world. She's a grown woman. She makes her own decisions. For some insane reason, she's decided to love you."

"Ah, I can't talk to you." Max started for the door.

"You're going to have to talk to me. We've got another assignment."

Max hesitated, turned, and went to the foot of the bed. "We?"

"You can't fire me if you're not my boss. Wouldn't want to miss out on that, would you?"

"Tempting."

"A ten-year-old boy has gone missing on the Oregon coast. Background is being sent to the command center. We'll leave as soon as I'm released. Should only be a day or two. Mostly bruised, nothing serious."

Jeremy could tell the inspector's mind had already started listing questions about the boy's disappearance.

"How about it?" Jeremy taunted.

"I'm leaving now." Max marched out of the hospital room.

"Excellent," Barnes muttered to himself. Now if he could only trick Max into marrying his pretty little assistant.

HE COULDN'T HELP himself. Max opened the envelope and glanced through the contents. Photographs of a little blond boy tugged at his heart.

Missing. Lost.

He studied the photograph, the boy's blue eyes calling out to him. They were young and hopeful, tinged with sadness.

They reminded him of Cassie's eyes.

He snapped the file closed. When she'd first started working for him he'd read melancholy in her eyes, but she'd covered it well with her smart-aleck comments and a sharp attitude. He'd bark orders, snap, even insult her at times. He'd been so devastated by his lost career and hovering madness. The only thing that relieved him was taking out his anger on the rest of the world.

He'd been brutal, for sure, and she'd taken it, and had given it back to him. She was tough all right. As the months passed the sadness had dissolved from her eyes, replaced by determination and even self-confidence. The more he'd dish out the more compassion she'd toss his way, like water on a flame.

For the first time in months, he'd been able to think straight, get his frame of reference, and lead a murder investigation.

Cassie had helped heal his wounds and brought him back to life. She'd even forced him to think about things, admit that he couldn't run from his madness anymore.

The only way to heal was to face it head-on, which he felt strong enough to do with her by his side.

Because she was strong, compassionate…

…and she loved him. She'd said so at the hospital.

Suddenly he knew what he had to do.

THE CAB pulled onto Cleveland Street and Cassie held her breath. Could she really do this? Knock on Mom's door after a year and a half? God, she was nervous, her palms sweating as she pulled a ten-dollar bill from her backpack.

She paid the cab driver and stepped out of the car. Standing on the sidewalk across the street, she studied the house, wishing that Max was with her.

Silly girl. She could do this on her own. She'd committed to doing everything on her own since her divorce.

Then she'd fallen in love with Max and it had seemed okay to share the burdens of life with another human being. The man she loved.

"Save that for Seattle," she said, knowing she could only deal with one highly emotional issue at a time.

Out of the corner of her eye she spotted someone get out of a car. She glanced up.

Max.

Frozen in place, she watched him walk across the street to her. The movement was fluid, as though his cane was a perfectly normal part of his body. He'd finally accepted it, she could tell.

He smiled. "Good afternoon, Miss Clarke."

He was here, supporting her when she needed him most.

"How about a little encouragement?" he said.

He pulled her against him and kissed her. A sob caught in the back of her throat. It was okay. Max was here, kissing her, offering encouragement and support.

And she welcomed it.

"I have something for you." He held out a shiny gold locket, similar to the one she'd lost in the abduction. "I thought you might want a replacement. For luck."

"It's beautiful," she said.

"Sorry, but I couldn't find fairy dust to put inside."

"That's okay." She wrapped her arms around him and squeezed. God, she loved this man.

"I'm scared," she said.

"Of seeing your mum?"

"What if she can't forgive me?"

He gripped her shoulders and looked into her eyes. "She loves you, Cassie. When someone loves you, they forgive you." He glanced at the ground. "I hope."

She studied his eyes. Did he mean…?

His gaze drifted up to meet hers. "Can you forgive me for being a complete idiot and pushing you away?"

"I love you. What do you think?"

"I think it's time I meet your mum."

"Me, too."

Happily ever after is just the beginning...
Turn the page for a sneak preview of
DANCING ON SUNDAY AFTERNOONS
by
Linda Cardillo

Harlequin Everlasting—
Every great love has a story to tell.™
A brand-new line from Harlequin Books
launching this February!

Prologue

Giulia D'Orazio
1983

I had two husbands—Paolo and Salvatore.

Salvatore and I were married for thirty-two years. I still live in the house he bought for us; I still sleep in our bed. All around me are the signs of our life together. My bedroom window looks out over the garden he planted. In the middle of the city, he coaxed tomatoes, peppers, zucchini—even grapes for his wine—out of the ground. On weekends, he used to drive up to his cousin's farm in Waterbury and bring back manure. In the winter, he wrapped the peach tree and the fig tree with rags and black rubber hoses against the cold, his massive, coarse hands gentling those trees as if they were his fragile-skinned babies. My neighbor, Dominic Grazza, does that for me now. My boys have no time for the garden.

In the front of the house, Salvatore planted roses. The

roses I take care of myself. They are giant, cream-colored, fragrant. In the afternoons, I like to sit out on the porch with my coffee, protected from the eyes of the neighborhood by that curtain of flowers.

Salvatore died in this house thirty-five years ago. In the last months, he lay on the sofa in the parlor so he could be in the middle of everything. Except for the two oldest boys, all the children were still at home and we ate together every evening. Salvatore could see the dining room table from the sofa, and he could hear everything that was said. "I'm not dead, yet," he told me. "I want to know what's going on."

When my first grandchild, Cara, was born, we brought her to him, and he held her on his chest, stroking her tiny head. Sometimes they fell asleep together.

Over on the radiator cover in the corner of the parlor is the portrait Salvatore and I had taken on our twenty-fifth anniversary. This brooch I'm wearing today, with the diamonds—I'm wearing it in the photograph also—Salvatore gave it to me that day. Upstairs on my dresser is a jewelry box filled with necklaces and bracelets and earrings. All from Salvatore.

I am surrounded by the things Salvatore gave me, or did for me. But, God forgive me, as I lie alone now in my bed, it is Paolo I remember.

Paolo left me nothing. Nothing, that is, that my family, especially my sisters, thought had any value. No house. No diamonds. Not even a photograph.

But after he was gone, and I could catch my breath from the pain, I knew that I still had something. In the middle of the night, I sat alone and held them in my hands, reading the words over and over until I heard his voice in my head. I had Paolo's letters.

* * * * *

Be sure to look for
DANCING ON SUNDAY AFTERNOONS
available January 30, 2007.
And look, too, for our other
Everlasting title available,
FALL FROM GRACE
by Kristi Gold.

FALL FROM GRACE
is a deeply emotional story of what a
long-term love really means.
As Jack and Anne Morgan discover,
marriage vows can be broken—
but they can be mended, too.
And the memories of their marriage have
an unexpected power to bring back a
love that never really left....

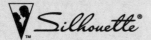